AF410778

Long Live the Sullied

The Sullied Warrior Duology (Book 2)

Also by Gaurav Sharma

God of the Sullied: The Sullied Warrior Duology (Book 1)
The Indian Story of an Author
Gone are the Days

Long Live the Sullied

The Sullied Warrior Duology (Book 2)

Gaurav Sharma

Think Tank Books™

First published in 2020 by Think Tank Books™, New Delhi
Website: thinktankbooks.com
Email: editorial@thinktankbooks.com

Gaurav Sharma asserts the moral right to be the author of this book.

Copyright © Think Tank Books™
Copyright Text © 2020 by **Gaurav Sharma**
Cover by **Devanshi Verma**

Illustrations by:
Mrinalini Sarkar (Fig. 1 & 2)
Gautam Arora (Fig. 5 & 6)
Adanyaa Garg (Fig. 3, 4, 7, 8, 9, 10, & 11)
Kirti Garg (Fig. 12, 13, 14, 15, 16, 17, 18, 19, & 20)

This is a work of fiction. Names, characters, places and incidents are either the product of the author's imagination or are used fictitiously, and any resemblance to any actual persons, living or dead, events or locales, is entirely coincidental.

ISBN: 978-81-936204-9-6
Price: INR 225/-
Maximum retail price of this book listed is only for the Indian subcontinent. Selling price may vary elsewhere.

10 9 8 7 6 5 4 3 2 1

Think Tank name & Think Tank logo are trademarks of Think Tank Books and its affiliates. Any unauthorised use is strictly prohibited.

Praise for 'Long Live the Sullied'

'A timeless adrenalin-pumping odyssey through ages and yet so apt statement on present times.'

- The Tribune

'An enthralling read that leaves you wanting more.'

- United News of India

'A timeless tale that flows like a movie. Every character is a hero in the story. It's a fiction aimed at humanizing relationships and elements of materialism.'

- Femonomic

This one is for you, Disha.

&

For all the readers of God of the Sullied.

About the Author

Gaurav Sharma is a Delhi-born, Bihar-raised and Canada-based writer, and founder of Think Tank Books. He studied business at Langara College, Vancouver and journalism at Guru Gobind Singh Indraprastha University, New Delhi.

After writing three textbooks related to mass communication, Gaurav authored *Gone are the Days* (semi-autobiographical fiction) in 2016, *The Indian Story of an Author* (creative nonfiction) and *God of the Sullied* (first book of the duology) in 2018. This novel, *Long Live the Sullied* is the sequel to *God of the Sullied*. Both stories in the duology would be translated in Hindi by Gaurav.

To know more, connect with the author on social media, reach out via his website authorgauravsharma.com, find him on Wikipedia or just Google his name. Something worth reading will come up, we promise!

Acknowledgements

This is my umpteenth attempt to writing acknowledgement - I am not exaggerating. For so many times, I just sat in front of my laptop, thinking about people who helped me create this novel the way it is now. No name came to my mind initially, for I believed it was me alone who made all of it possible. A bit more introspection revealed how self-obsessed I can become at times and that there had been so many creative minds that came together to help me in some way or the other to turn my book into reality. I can't thank enough these lovely people, but I'll try anyway!

Ishani, for editorially helping me with the first book of the duology, God of the Sullied and for giving me the idea of writing a sequel to it. So here it is - Long Live the Sullied!

Devanshi, for conceptualizing and designing such a beautiful cover for the novel. Girl, your art is magical! I wish there could be different covers made by you for each copy of this novel & all my upcoming books in print. I know it doesn't work like that, but that's how much I loved it. Let's catch up when I am in Delhi & keep in touch, will ya?

Kirti, for taking out time to read both the novels and creating nine elegant illustrations for this one, despite having end term exams approaching. Thank you very much for what you have done for me.

Adanyaa, for making seven beautiful illustrations for the novel and for promoting God of the Sullied & Long Live the Sullied whenever and wherever you could. I wish you all the best for your future ventures.

Mrinalini, for creating the first two beautiful illustrations in the book. I hope to see you as an established dentist soon.

Gautam, for designing two illustrations. Your contribution is very much appreciated.

Inderjeet, for trying to withdraw time to beta read the manuscript. Also, thanks for everything!

Sahil, for taking out time to read God of the Sullied and for trying to design the cover for this one.

Jupinderjit, for sharing your valuable review for this novel. I hope your books become widely read.

Jaison, for withdrawing time to review my book(s). Your support is highly appreciated.

My cousin Tanya, for putting her time and zeal in promotion and sales for God of the Sullied. I wish you the best in your life.

Luvy, for sharing the feedback on initial drafts of this novel & for writing about my books on Femonomic.

Thank you! Dr. Ravi Dhar, Dr. Neeru Johri, Dr. Ritu Sood, Dr. Kiran Bala, Dr. Neha Jain, Dr. Mukti Sanyal, Dr. Rachita Rana and entire teaching & administration fraternity along with amazing students at JIMS, Sharda University, K.R. Mangalam University, IITM and Bharati College for promoting literature and encouraging reading. I thank you all for your support.

Rashmi, for taking care of the tax works for this otherwise poor author. Could you tweak some paperwork and make me rich on papers somehow? Never mind.

Ranbijay, for writing the blurb. I know it's too early to know if readers would buy the book after reading what you wrote there, but I'll mention your name, just in case!

Leema, for just being there in my sub-conscious and occupying the most valuable space there is, for no reason!

My brother Aman, for everything but book-related. I don't know if you would ever help me distribute and promote my books, but you are wonderful, nonetheless.

Chunnu and Chhotu, for being there, doing nothing. One of you must be happy to see your so-called real name on dedication page.

Thank you! Dear readers of my books. Now it's time for you to make The Sullied Warrior Duology a bestseller, turning me into a super-rich author!

Last but not least… ~~I would like to thank God.~~ Err, I am an atheist.

Ladies & gentleman, boys & girls, journalists, bloggers, students, lovers & haters, I conclude The Sullied Warrior Duology with Long Live the Sullied. Happy Reading!

Glossary

Acharya : Teacher / Preceptor

Advaita-Vedanta : A religious principle to spiritual realisation

Amma : An older woman (proper noun in the book)

Atman : Soul / Real self

Aum / Om : Most sacred mantra of God in Hinduism

Avatar : Manifestation of a deity

Bhogi : A commoner / Enjoyer of worldly aspirations

Brahman : The highest universal principle / God

Brahmin : One of the social classes in Hinduism

Brahm-Kshatriya : A person with traits of Brahmin and Kshatriya

Choupal : Community space in (Indian) villages

Dhoti : Traditional men's garment in India

Gurukul : Educational institution / Learning centre

Ji : Suffix used with names to denote respect

Jyotish : Astrology

Jyotish-Acharya : Astrologer

Kali : The evil

Kali-Yuga : Era of the evil (last age per Hindu scriptures)

Kathopanishad : One of the primary Upanishads

Kshatriya : One of the social classes in Hinduism

Kutcha : (Something in) raw state / Crude

Maa	: Mother
Maha-Mantri	: Chief Minister of the kingdom
Maha-Purohit	: High priest
Maharaj	: Colloquial word for the king
Matha	: Religious monastery in Hinduism
Maya	: Illusion created by supernatural powers
Moksha	: Liberation / Freedom from the cycle of rebirth
Nirvana	: Synonym of moksha in Buddhism
Padmasana	: Lotus position in yoga
Panchayat	: Village council
Pundit	: An expert (in religious practices)
Purohit	: Priest
Rogi	: Sick person
Sadhana	: Practices leading to spiritual perfection
Samsara	: World / Cycle of rebirth
Sannyasa	: Ascetics
Sari	: Traditional women's garment in India
Sarpanch Ji	: Head of the village council
Sat-Yuga	: Golden age (first of the four ages per Hinduism)
Shloka	: Category of verse in Sanskrit poetry / scriptures
Upanishad	: Part of the Vedas (philosophy of Hinduism)
Vaidya	: Medic / Physician
Vedanta	: School of Hindu philosophy
Yajna	: Offering / Ritual done in front of a sacred fire
Yogi	: A person proficient in yoga / meditation

Time

Rudraputra Royal Palace: Present

The royal guards stood at the hinged heavy metallic door, holding spears in their hands to prevent anyone without authorisation from entering the palace that had always been open to the public for meeting with the cabinet and Eklavya - the king of Rudraputra. Something catastrophic happened last night that doomed the kingdom, immediately resulting in restricted access policy in effect, keeping all outsiders from entering unless accompanying any minister or the King himself. And it was for the same reason why the guards resisted *Acharya* Virbhadra from entering the palace to go meet the King.

Acharya was refused entry for the second time, the first being just a few days ago. Despite identifying himself as Eklavya's guru, he was given yet another reason for the denial – the previous was the absence of the king in the palace. Seemed as if the royal palace didn't want to welcome *Acharya* inside its huge doors. If he wanted, he would have entered forcefully as his might was way immense than those two guards standing at the door, but Virbhadra didn't want to create any chaos. And so, he kept on requesting the guards, again and again, to let him through, only to get their refusal each time.

Fig. 1: Acharya Virbhadra walking towards palace doors.

One thing was for sure that *Acharya* Virbharda would not return without meeting Eklavya this time. It was too much work and time that he already put to reach that close to Eklavya, his favourite student of all time. The argument between *Acharya* and the guards went on for long until *Maha-Mantri* arrived from outside the palace on his chariot, non-verbally commanding the guards to open the doors for his entry. The guards gave way to *Maha-Mantri's* chariot the moment they saw his signal. As the chariot treaded inside the palace, Virbhadra called *Maha-Mantri*, shouting out loud in a requesting tone. *Maha-Mantri* stopped and looked at *Acharya* with a thoughtful gaze.

A *yogi* in his simple, plain, peasant-styled clothes, wearing wooden sabots on his feet and standing at the door of the palace with hands folded posed no threat to the king and to the palace. And so, *Maha-Mantri* got off from his chariot and came closer, asking *Acharya* what the matter was. Virbhadra, upon revealing his identity as the guru of Eklavya in the mountain-*Gurukul* was asked by *Maha-Mantri* to accompany him inside. Though *Maha-Mantri* never saw *Acharya* before, he had heard a lot of good things about him from Eklavya.

Royal guards who stood like a garrison between *Acharya* and the palace earlier, now made way for him, bending their heads down in respect.

While on his way to the royal court, *Acharya* asked *Maha-Mantri* about what was it that tormented the palace in a sudden span of one night? Why Eklavya was called immediately to the palace and why everyone including *Maha-Mantri* looked so tensed?

Maha-Mantri looked at *Acharya*, telling him to see for himself what happened last night and made him realise that he arrived at the palace at the wrong time. He also attested that whatever was inside had already made many workers and ministers lose their wits at the very sight of it, cautioning *Acharya* to be prepared to endure the gore he was about to witness. Despite being a fierce warrior and a *yogi*, Virbhadra felt a chill in his spine as he entered the hallway to the royal court.

What was it that doomed the state of Rudraputra? Why was Eklavya called immediately to the palace? What gore *Maha-Mantri* talked about with *Acharya* Virbhadra? And what made people who witnessed it lose their senses? Only time would reveal…

~~~***~~~
~~~

Pundir

"Hey! Senior, Senior! Everyone's out there. Students, the consortium, and *Acharya* Virbhadra too," I instantly gestured with my hand, deterring him from speaking any further. Being afraid of my anger, he ran away from my dorm. It was a little kid whom I saw a couple of times before, roaming around the campus and attending archery sessions. I didn't want to be disturbed during my meditation. It was a big day for me, and I prepared my mind to seize it, I knew I would; I had to.

I opened my eyes while remaining in *padmasana*, taking heavy breaths and feeling a weird sensation in my gut. Not that I was going to fight for the first time, I combated against countless trained warriors and won over each of them, every single time. It was only Eklavya who beat me once in the archery test when we both were young and learning. Eklavya, my best friend and the scion of Ikshvaku. My 16-years long apprenticeship in *Gurukul* under *Acharya* Virbhadra and *Acharya* Bhushan turned me into a *Brahm-Kshatriya*, a mindful war machine.

If Lord Parashurama had been in *Kali-Yuga*, he would be much like me; a prudent sage with fierce combat skills.

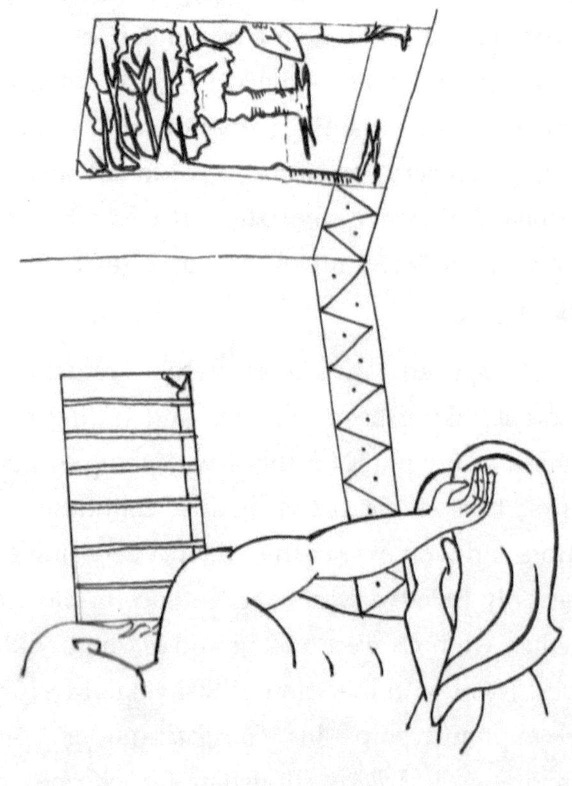

Fig. 2: Pundir in Padmasana, little kid at the door.

I ended *padmasana* and stood up while folding my hands before the wall-hung portrait of Adi Shankaracharya, our founding guru. Underneath, there was an earthen pot filled with water, which I could see my reflection in. I looked tensed and nervous, as anybody would be if they were going to fight with *Acharya* Virbhadra. I put on the headband that was awarded to me after achieving the highest student-rank for excelling in combat in the *Gurukul*. I was trained there for the most prolonged duration due to some most robust cruelties life could fling at me. I was the only student in his early thirties that was still learning in the *Gurukul*. I had to fight a battle in the future, a fight with the evil, a crusade to free my family and village from the clutches of the darkness. I wanted to become as good as, or even better, way better than *Acharya* Virbhadra.

Acharya Virbhadra and *Acharya* Bhushan were to teach us for the first three years in the *Gurukul*. However, my humble requests of letting them be my teachers for as long as I wanted and furthering my stay in the *Gurukul* was accepted by the consortium, and I was given permission to learn all fighting skills until I felt I mastered them completely. And without a doubt, I mastered and remastered everything they could teach me there.

I walked out of my room, having prepared my mind for the fight. Students had just finished their morning prayer in the ground. I saw all of them and staff sitting around the stage, eagerly waiting for my arrival in the field. Most of them, however, cheered for *Acharya*, as everybody was excited to see him fight. It was going to be a rarest of the rare event in the *Gurukul*.

***

Acharya's appearance was spellbound, especially on that day. I felt his eyes filled with ferocious enchantment in them. He had long matted hair as though it was an ornament given to him by Lord Shiva. Broad chest and muscular arms that were barely fitting into the iron armour he wore that day. Tall frame with every bone as dense as his armour itself. Sinewy muscles and protruding shoulders that complemented his well-crafted torso.

Acharya Virbhadra had curbed ageing. I had been seeing him like that for the past 16 years. My seniors and even their seniors saw him as-is from even longer ago – when the time was still young, as they say. His decades-long practice of meditation, *sadhana* and exercise led him to attain an ageless growth.

I bent my head down with hands folded to seek his blessings before fighting with him and said, "I bow to you, *Acharya*."

"May He who is not, bless you the victory over me in this test," *Acharya* spoke merrily.

I wondered if he had developed some secret plans to beat me in the fight. "What's the reason behind your radiant smile this morning? If I may ask."

"I am glad you asked, son," he said with his head held high, "this morning shall bring certain victory to me."

"But *Acharya*, you just blessed me the victory over you in the test. How can you and I both win the fight?" I couldn't get his contradictory statement.

Acharya now had an even broader smile on his face. "If I win, I'll be happy for an obvious reason for winning over you as a warrior. If you win, I'll win as your guru. Being your guru, I indeed want you to win today, Pundir! Seeing one's student excelling themselves is one of the proudest and happiest moments for a teacher. What else I can ask for?" He explained.

I was relieved after hearing him say that. The consortium signalled us to begin duelling with swords.

The crowd cheered for both of us now. *Acharya* took his position with the double-edged sword maintained at his eye level, just as he taught me. But his precision was way better than mine. Morning sun rays reflected from the edge of the shiny sword that was held in *Acharya's* right hand, proving his bravery that invited others to find their own hidden courage in the battle of life.

I glanced around as the crowd became silent suddenly. Students were awestruck after seeing *Acharya's* initial move of delicately slashing the sword in the air. Just as a cobra swings its hood in attacking position. He was all set to charge, waiting for me to take my stance.

I knew I had to do something else to win, or at least be on par with him in the fight. Defeating *Acharya* by his own teachings to me was impossible. I took my position, drawing an arc on the ground with my right foot while bringing it near the left one and holding my sword with both the hands. Students cheered wildly again, shouting my name out loud and praising my unprecedented move. My sword had a tight leather-rope grip which *Acharya's* sword lacked in. I was glad I worked on that grip last night.

Both of us had an unreadable face, devoid of any expression that could give slight hints to each other about our next move.

I charged on *Acharya* with a mighty roar. He dodged to the side swiftly. I swivelled in his direction, changing the angle of my sword. *Acharya* ducked that too. I was not at all surprised by his subtle fluid moves of defending himself. He wanted to let me try everything I had got, it seemed to be such.

Acharya quickly thrust his sword towards me only to be met by my sword. Squeaky sounds emerged from the friction of the metal. He then leapt on me like a jaguar, but his swift move was a little slow this time, giving me ample time to stoop down and reach the other side. Attacking and defending kept on for a while until I heard my heart pounding vigorously, but *Acharya* looked as subtle as he was before the fight had commenced. He smirked, summoning me to give in all that I had got from him.

Our attack and defensive moves soared once again. I knew I might not survive for long before *Acharya's* endurance, but I wanted to take my chances.

The fresh morning air was just as perfect for keeping our body temperature under control.

There was a commotion hustling inside my mind, an uncontrollable urge of defeating *Acharya* at any cost. If my desperate want of winning over him were visible, the air would have been crimson that morning. No sooner had I thrust my sword towards *Acharya's* neck did his sword slightly penetrate my armour by the abdomen. I felt mild pain and saw another slash come for my chest.

It wasn't time to think and fight by the rules. If I hadn't done anything at that very moment, I would have lost the fight right there, right then! Before *Acharya's* sword came any closer to my chest, I threw mine at his foot and pretended as if it slipped through my hand. *Acharya's* foot began bleeding, and the consortium immediately halted the fight. Students went into utter silence; the consortium was concerned about *Acharya's* bleeding.

"I take no pride in winning over you, Pundir. I was waiting to see your better warrior-side," *Acharya* made me realise what I had done while looking at his bleeding foot that was turned deep red. I was nervous and frightened at the same time, but *Acharya* delicately smiled at me as if he knew that I threw my sword intentionally at his foot.

Though I was aware in my heart of hearts that he was never going to hit me with the sword, yet I couldn't afford to lose. It was never about the pain or taking hits but victory and only victory.

The consortium declared the result as undecided, and one thing became for sure, that I was not going to fight with *Acharya* Virbhadra ever again. Part of me was happy to escape from the embarrassment of losing in front of everyone, and at the same time, I regretted my wrong action in the fight.

I now realise that it was the day *Kali* began trapping me into its clutches. Students dismissed for their breakfast and after that for their classes, and I desired to go to my dorm and take rest to rejuvenate my mind for an upcoming test that was a religious debate with *Acharya* Bhushan later that day.

***

Fig. 3: Swordfight between Pundir & Virbhadra.

Soon after coming into my dorm, I took a bath in the pond to freshen up, easing off the exhaustion that fight had developed. I ate my breakfast with remaining students and staff as most of them were done eating while I bathed. After eating my food, I sat down to quickly go through some books of *Advaita Vedanta*. I had no clue about what *Acharya* Bhushan might ask me during the debate.

I memorised and to the best of my knowledge, understood all the Brahma Sutras and Bhagavad Gita by heart, yet every time I read them, they felt new to me. There was so much to learn from those scriptures that a single human life seemed not enough to understand the depth of their knowledge. Only a handful like Adi Shankaracharya and *Acharya* Bhushan knew the real meaning of those sacred texts. What I knew and learned from Bhushanacharya would make up a tiny fraction of the immense knowledge contained in the scriptures of *Advaita Vedanta*.

Even though I was regarded as an excellent student of theology in *Gurukul*, I knew I was not the best! It was Eklavya who best understood and implemented the sacred teachings of the *Vedanta* and its philosophies into life.

Besides, traces of that epic debate between Eklavya and *Acharya* Bhushan, and later with *Acharya* Kaushal were still fresh in *Gurukul's* air. It was when he left us to visit his family after spending three years in the *Gurukul*.

Eklavya was the only student who got the headband for excelling in theology, and that too in mere three years of education. He never came back after that. It didn't matter to me much as I focused on mastering my martial arts and combat skills, and my headband was the ultimate proof of me being the best of the beasts in combat.

Philosophies and principles never settled conflicts in *Kali-Yuga*. One needs to know the use of force and might to conquer evil. And I was going to do just that. I would free my village from the fear of death, teaching fellow villagers how to fight for their rights and lives. I would not spare those who harassed my family and took away peace from us.

I was there with Eklavya in the chariot, going downhill to visit my family. We were happy and excited to go see our families after three years, assuring each other of our meeting in the *Gurukul* after three months.

I, then at the age of sixteen was totally unaware of what future had to offer me. I returned to the *Gurukul* after five years, and found out that Eklavya never came back!

During my five-year stay at the village, I realised I was too weak to fight the bandits. I needed more rigorous training so that I could train my people to combat with those hill bandits and end their sufferings. Thus, I went back to the *Gurukul*. After listening to my concerns, the consortium accepted me again. *Acharya* Virbhadra assured me the best of his combat training, and he delivered his promise well enough.

Lost profoundly in the spiritual acumen of *Kathopanishad*, I didn't realise how the day went by. I looked out of the window with my eyes steady to the horizon. The sun changed its colour from yellow to orange and glowingly collided with the skyline. I closed the *Upanishad* and put it in its place, thanking almighty for all the wisdom I attained from studying theology.

The time had come to test my knowledge of those holy books that I garnered during a total of thirteen years of my education. It was the time *Acharya* Bhushan would debate with me to test my religious and spiritual understanding of the self, this universe and the God. I was ready to put forward my philosophies and perspective of seeing life and true-self.

I walked out of my dorm, having prepared my mind to answer each question *Acharya* Bhushan would ask. What's more, I developed some of my arguments to trick *Acharya*. Little did I know that it was going to be the fiercest debate I would ever participate in. Moreover, satisfactorily answering all his questions alone would be a significant accomplishment, forget about making counter-arguments to *Acharya*. But it was going to be my last debate with him, so I didn't want to keep anything inside my mind.

All these years of *sadhana* and meditation taught me one thing that is vital for achieving *Nirvana*. That human mind continuously forms deceptive concepts and desires that keep on floating at an elusive distance, and as you go further to catch them, they recede back away from you. Those who put their valuable life in the chasing of such worldly desires are staunch fools.

***

The chamber was filled with the students, the consortium and the staff. *Acharya* Bhushan sat opposite to the mat kept on the floor for me to perch.

I smelled the kerosene fuming out of the lamps hung on the timber poles. Seemed as if the fire digested all the evil, emitting ceaseless puffs of black smoke from it. Those lamps threw their beams of yellow light in all directions. Calm and soothing wind of that night, gliding inside through the windows was enough to flicker the flames of the lamps.

I climbed on the platform and sat on my mat facing *Acharya* Bhushan. It was not the first time I debated with him, yet I felt a sensation in my body that was completely strange. I was nervous, hopeful, cautious and active at the same time. *Acharya* passed a decent smile, in response, I folded my hands and bowed to him. I looked around for *Acharya* Virbhadra and found him sitting beside the consortium. He smiled at me, assuring his foot was alright now. I was a bit relieved. But then I saw Kaushalacharya sitting next to *Acharya* Virbhadra, and that was enough to put me back in the same stressed state as I was before.

How could I forget *Acharya* Kaushal's questions to Eklavya that were not only difficult to answer but also required an exceptional understanding of the complicated scriptures of *Vedanta*? I bowed to him too, only to get a cold response that was very well expected of him.

No one could ever understand what his problem was with those students whom he never taught.

"Pundir, I hope you are well prepared for this debate," said *Acharya* Bhushan.

I affirmed, "Absolutely! *Acharya*."

The consortium signalled us to begin our debate. It was *Acharya* who would open the debate, asking the first question, and upon answering, I would put forth my question, and the debate would proceed likewise. Whoever stops responding would lose. Besides, anyone from the audience and the consortium could counter-question or ask for further explanation from *Acharya* and me.

Acharya opened the debate with his weird question, "Who are you?" It took a few moments for me to register what he asked. Had it been a typical day, I would have answered it by telling my name and introducing myself a little bit. But it never worked like that in theology debates. I had seen students failing their tests because they underestimated the complexity of these simple questions. I didn't want any counter-argument, and so I replied, "I am the reflection of my consciousness."

"What consciousness are you talking about? Is it your mind or body, or both?" *Acharya* supplemented his question.

"I am the reflection of my consciousness. Consciousness is exclusive of all body-mind realms. I am neither my body nor its psychological functions nor senses nor mind, and I am not emptiness either.

I accumulated my body over a while and gathered the contents of my mind from the outside world. What is gathered or collected is mine but can't be me. My body is known to me, and I can define its characteristics. Besides, I know how my body transformed over all these years. And if I can witness the changes happening with my body, I can't be the body itself. There is something else that knows the changes occurring without itself undergoing the transformation. Those who associate themselves with the characteristics of their bodies are ignorant and weak to discover their true self.

The psychological functions of my body are known to me as well, for I can feel when I am hungry or sick or tired. I know when my thirst comes and goes, I feel when my hunger comes and goes. Since I know both the presence and absence of my psychological functions, I can't be those either.

I feel because my skin feels, I see because my eyes see, and I hear because my ears hear. I, in fact, know when my eyes are seeing, skin is feeling or ears are hearing. I realise when my senses function or not function. Thus, I am not my senses as well.

I am not emotions, memories or intellect. I observe the coming and going of my feelings. I can recall or forget the memories of the past. Also, my intelligence is the result of the cognition that is based on tangible and intangible objects. Intellect comes, goes, expands and shrinks. This proves that I am neither emotions nor memories nor intellect.

I am also not emptiness as I am not non-existent. If I can witness the changes in my body, if I can realise my body's psychological functions, if I can recall my memories, grow my intellect, hear, see, think and act, I am indeed not void. Therefore, I am not emptiness.

The truth is that I am consciousness. The consciousness that is independent of all these conditions and body-mind-senses. Consciousness does not depend on anything, and thus, it is the truth of the self. It is me, it is you, *Acharya* and it is all of us, and all of us are it."

"Brilliant! Pundir. Brilliant! Brilliant!" All the students, the consortium along with *Acharya* Bhushan appreciated my explanation. I was surprised by the sublimest wisdom I showed there. It came naturally though.

"*Acharya*, could you please tell me what *Maya* is all about?" I asked *Acharya*. Part of me was laughing at myself as asking such questions would not at all put him in deep thinking. But it was my turn to put up a question and not asking anything was more embarrassing than asking fundamental inquiries related to *Vedanta*, so I went ahead and questioned him. He smiled, assuring me he would answer it in the most perfect way possible. I was very well expecting that reaction from him.

"*Maya* is an illusion. It is the ultimate form of ignorance. *Maya* is present since the time immemorial. No one really knows when it began or why it exists. What we know about it is that it diminishes at the dawn of your consciousness - the very consciousness that you just talked about, son. As your knowledge of the true-self becomes profound, *Maya* ceases to exist. We tend to identify ourselves with the characteristics of our body, thoughts in our mind, ego, hatred and worldly desires rather than *atman*, the true-self. This ignorance alone is *Maya*.

Maya can be compared to the clouds in the night sky, and consciousness represents the stars. Stars are already there in the sky, but clouds obstruct our vision. When the clouds disperse, we become aware that stars have been there all the time. So, *Maya* – the clouds appearing as selfishness, hatred, egotism, lust, greed, anger, ambition and love vanish as we meditate, introspect, engage in unselfish acts through purity, self-restraint, contentment and truthfulness. Upon breakage of this delusionary ignorance, *Maya*, all that is left is consciousness or *Brahman*."

"Excellent! Excellent!" Everyone applauded *Acharya's* explanation. I never felt that *Acharya* Bhushan was debating with me, seemed as if he was teaching in the class. Most debates in the *Gurukul* and anywhere for that matter had some competitiveness and intention of winning the argument. But I never saw *Acharya* Bhushan competing to succeed in any spiritual debate he took part in. He never boasted his profound knowledge of scriptures and *Vedanta* philosophies. Perhaps, that was why he was unbeatable in theology.

Acharya asked something that I was not comfortable answering about,

"What is *Moksha*? And how do you attain it?"

I still hadn't been able to convince my mind about how *Moksha* could be attained. I wasn't sure if achieving *Moksha* would ever be possible in the age of *Kali*. It was not that I didn't know its concept and theory, I was very well versed with its inception and reception in society. But I often found it hard to comply with its principles itself. And I was not in favour of vouching or preaching about something that I was myself not sure about.

All those years of training and education had taught me that *Moksha* is the ultimate liberation from *Maya*. *Maya*, the illusion that affects everything in the universe. I was not sure if I would ever be able to attain *Moksha*. One needs to shed all human feelings and emotions to liberate from *Maya* and achieve the highest consciousness. I couldn't do away with the sense of love for my family, friends and dear ones, hatred for those who deserved it, greed for more knowledge and strength, anger for adversities in life, the joy of success and fear of failure. Now that *Acharya* had asked me that question, I was left with two choices. Either, I would refuse to answer and lose the debate right there right then, or I would try explaining something that I was not fully aware of, somewhat not convinced of. I chose the latter as losing was just not an option. Before *Acharya* Kaushal and the consortium confronted me about not answering the question I responded.

"*Moksha* is the liberation and release of one's soul from the *samsara*, the cycle of birth and death and re-birth. *Moksha* is the highest goal of the soul. *Moksha* frees the soul from being affected by the laws of karma. It is achieved when all our karma is exhausted, and there remains nothing to act or ponder upon. Anything that is a result of our thought, action or reaction can't be eternal like *Moksha*, which is the constant and inherent essence of the soul.

One can attain *Moksha* by surrendering their ignorance. Ignorance here means not realising the true-self, associating *atman* with physical characteristics, believing in materialistic things and failing to understand what *Maya* is. There are several *yogic* techniques to silence the noise inside our mind and body. To attain liberation, one must dwell upon true-self by cleansing the thoughts. Thoughts lead to the manifestation of good and bad karma, and karma won't let one attain liberation. *Vedanta* says 'I am that one' which means we all are *Brahman*, we all have God inside us. All that is required to attain *Moksha* is to muzzle the noise and connect with the source present inside you."

"Splendid! Splendid!" The consortium cheered for me. What I presented was rhetoric that was taught to me in previous classes by *Acharya* Bhushan. He intended to make me understand what *Moksha* is all about. However, I always found it impossible to grasp the very fundamentals of the principles of attaining liberation. My consciousness never agreed with this philosophy.

What would remain in life if we give up everything? What's the meaning of living if we have no desires, no willingness, no feelings, no thoughts, no actions and reactions? I once again questioned myself in my mind. The audience cheered yet I was not happy to falsely testify what seemed impractical to me.

Now it was my turn to put up a question. Something was not feeling right. I developed a hunch that someone from the consortium would counter me on my explanation of *Moksha*. I would have asked the toughest of the tough questions, I would have requested *Acharya* to recite difficult *shlokas* from the *Upanishads*, I would have done something to prove my knowledge of the scriptures only if *Acharya* Kaushal could keep himself from interfering. Even before I could utter something, he spoke and ruined all my strategies to get an edge over *Acharya* Bhushan.

"You know so much about attaining *Moksha*. The way you beautifully explained everything is beyond what I expected of you, Pundir. I am amazed at your knowledge of theology and *Vedanta*. Even those who are far more experienced than you fail to understand the concept of *Moksha* in its entirety. My respect and salute to *Acharya* Bhushan for giving you such priceless gem of knowledge of the scriptures." I could not believe my ears for some time. 'How come he is praising me?' I thought in my mind.

"But, what's the point of excelling in theory without even trying a hand at its implementation? You, knowing how to attain liberation and not doing anything to accomplish it are as good as someone having the ability to see but not willing to open their eyes. What's the meaning of taking enlightenment from *Acharya* if it does not drive you from inside to seek true-self? Tell me, son. Why are you, after gaining more than a decade of education still thinking of avenging the hill-bandits? When would you begin your journey of seeking *Moksha*?

Why don't you leave behind all the misery and free yourself from the clutches of karma? Why winning at everything by hook or crook matters so much to you? Which Pundir is the real one? The one who has grudges and lives in constant fear of failure or the one who just spoke about consciousness, *Brahman*, *Maya* and *Moksha*? The consortium and everybody present here want to know when will you be spiritually awakened, what is that you are chasing in this material and the mortal world, and why it is that your appetite for vengeance is growing?..."

At first, I felt the silence and after that arose murmuring among the audience. I froze to the ground, feeling a weird sensation in my body and electric currents behind the ears. *Acharya* Kaushal was still speaking, but I couldn't recognise his speech. All I heard was a beeping sound emerging out from inside my ears. His questions made my head spin, mouth slightly open and loose, and my eyes kept on wandering in an unknown direction. Nausea cramped my stomach. I felt as if my intestines were floating inside my body. The consortium stared at me, leaving my mind confused. Seemed as if thick layers of cloud took over my mind and I felt a painful lump on the back of my throat as my eyes began tearing.

My breathing became shallow, and I felt a sharp pain in the top nerve of my brain. I felt everything was fading away in front of me. Or maybe it was my vision going blurry. I wanted to take off my clothes despite the chilly winds blowing in through the windows. I sweated profusely yet felt a chill in my blood. My head swam with regrets of answering to *Acharya* Bhushan's previous question about *Moksha*. It would have been better if I just had not replied. I was emptied from inside, feeling my pulse pounding and legs shaking. I wanted to run away from the chamber but could not gather the courage and strength to stand up and move.

I had no choice left but to face Kaushalacharya's striking comments and questions somehow. With tears flowing out of my eyes and my hands folded, I sobbingly spoke my heart out.

"The sole purpose of gaining an education in the *Gurukul* was to help my fellow beings, my family and friends. What's wrong with it? I do respect *Acharya's* teachings, but I am not yet ready to seek liberation. Why is this unacceptable? *Acharya* Kaushal, it is my dharma to fight those who are evil, and I will continue to do that in this life. Maybe, in next life, I shall try to seek *Moksha*. Why I am not allowed to do it? As far as my emotions and feelings are concerned, I can tell you that those are as human as I am. I love my dear ones, I have hatred for those who put others down, anger for those who deserve my wrath, greed to earn more power, strength and intelligence, and respect for those who treat me with respect. I can't embrace good without imagining evil, I can't value knowledge without acknowledging ignorance, I can't win without competing, and it is hard for me to seek true-self without empathising with other living beings first.

How can I neglect these essential emotions that make me human? How can I not regard the principle of duality in this universe? I pledge before you all to finish those who killed my people and continue to exploit my village and its resources. Those who come even close to my family in bad faith will lose their life. I can't let *Kali* span its wings swiftly, not until I am alive. In this battle, I am willing to give up everything I learned about theology and philosophies. I think I am going to need my fighting skills more than my philosophies of *Vedanta*. Despite being a *Brahmin*, I must fight for justice like a *Kshatriya* does - just as Lord Parashurama did to avenge the killers of his father.

With utmost respect to *Acharya* Bhushan for his teachings, I seek his blessings. The knowledge he gave me will bear its fruits for sure. I can't thank enough *Acharya* Virbhadra, *Acharya* Bhushan and all of you for treating me as one of your own. I gracefully accept my defeat in this test of ideologies and philosophies. I will leave for my village early morning tomorrow and don't wish to come back here, ever." With my head bent down, I headed swiftly to my dorm.

Seemed as if I had taken a massive load off my mind. Nobody said anything to me, but they all were shocked by my confession, and I really didn't care what everyone thought about me then.

***

The moon was almost over my head, and I knew it was a little before midnight. Time went by so quickly in the chamber. I came inside my dorm, shut the door and began packing my belongings in a cloth bag. I folded the wall-hung portrait of Adi Shankaracharya and kept it aside. I didn't want to take it with me as it would always remind me of my last day at *Gurukul,* which I never wanted to recall. I was tired, but I knew it would be a rough night for me to peacefully sleep. Moreover, I had to leave in few hours as Gandharv would bring the chariot even before the sunrise.

Gandharv was an old man who operated the chariot service on the mountain. He returned every three months to deliver his service for one day. I saw him following the same routine ever since I came to the *Gurukul*.

Part of me was excited to leave behind everything that happened there and see my family after a long, long time while another part of me worried speculating about the present condition of the outside world. I had no idea what my village looked like, how my parents would be, what condition my neighbours would be in. Laying on the ground, thinking deeply about what just happened in the chamber, I never realised when I went into a deep slumber.

I woke up to the drumming of the raindrops falling on the roof of my dorm and realised it was time to get ready. Everything was already packed. I washed my face, drank some water and held my bag. I felt as if I was leaving behind something mine knowingly. I saw that rolled-up portrait of Shankaracharya and picked it up, I also picked up my knife that was with me from the times I first came to the *Gurukul*, I put that in my bag too. I don't know why I put the portrait suddenly.

After a while, the rain subsided, it was more of a drizzle. Most of the students were still sleeping, those who were awake lined up to use the bathrooms, few who had to leave were taking their luggage out, *Acharya* Virbhadra and *Acharya* Bhushan were already meditating in their sheds. I bowed to them from a distance. They probably were not aware of me bowing to them as their eyes were closed. I saw the chariot outside the gate. Gandharv was on time as usual.

I turned around before sitting into the chariot, filling up in my eyes the last glimpse of the *Gurukul*. I stood there for a moment, possibly recalling each day I spent there. A sudden nostalgic breeze hit me in my chest as it felt heavy.

"Are you coming, Pundir?" shouted Gandharv and I resumed my walk towards the chariot. I sat inside and saw three more students gazing strangely at me. They were inside the chamber last night, I remember. I pretended to ignore their presence.

Gandharv patted on the back of both the horses, "C'mon! Boys, show us what you've got," pulling their rope gently. Both of them neighed, and the chariot descended downhill. That day marked my second birth. With hope in my heart and questions in my mind, I braced myself for a future utterly unknown to me.

~~~***~~~
~~~

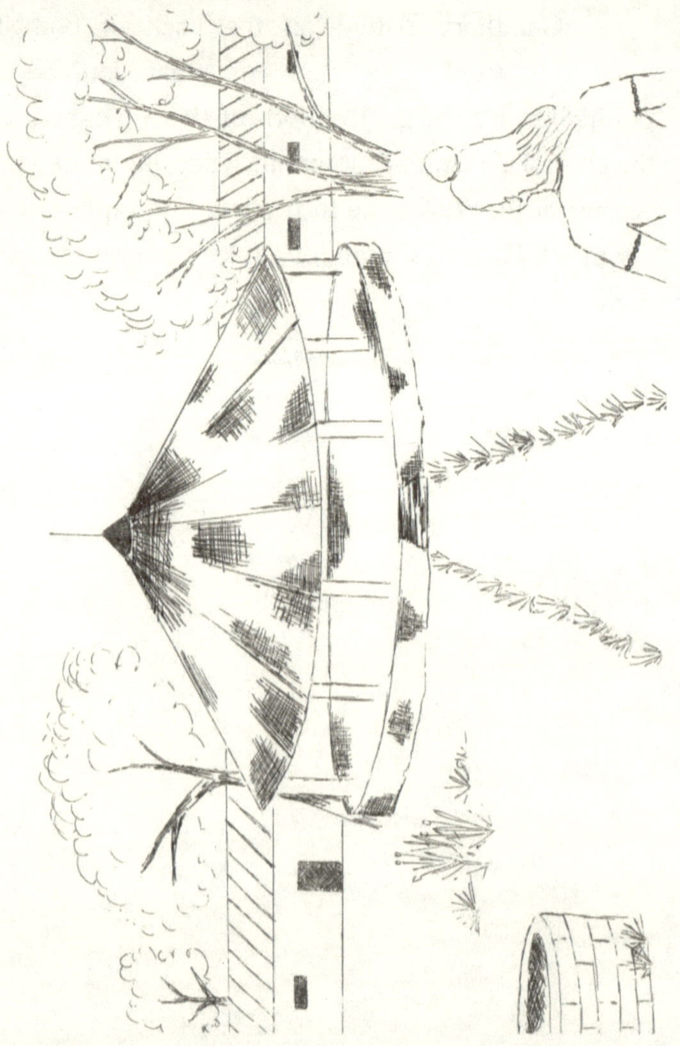

Fig. 4: Pundir embracing last glimpse of his Gurukul.

Maha-Purohit

After confessing to Eklavya about my wrongful deeds of killing him even before his birth, I probably became the only person in Rudraputra who despite being evil, was granted his life and freedom back. It was perhaps my good karma in the past that spared my life from being ended in the cemetery on the confession day. After about a decade of my confession now, I still hold myself guilty of the murder of Sumati, *Amma* and eventually Vyas.

I knew I didn't deserve to live anymore. But now that Eklavya spared me for my sins, I made sure I repay him and work for the righteous until my last breath. This would certainly not undo my past but give me a reason for living my remaining life, and strength to die in lesser vain. Maybe, doing the rightful was my way of attaining karmic redemption.

I was born in a Brahmin family living in a small village in Kashi. Childbirth was celebrated in our small village with great enthusiasm. *Purohits* conducted *yajna*, villagers collectively organised feasts for several days, and every local and foreigner would be cordially invited to be a part of the celebration. Religious ceremonies commenced as per the faith of the clan in which the children were born. People dressed up in the fanciest clothes and danced as if they are dancing for the last time in their lives. Ceremonies seemed like a riot of colours, music and scent, making everyone hyper with excitement. But the day I was born brought mourning in the village. No *purohit* or *pundit* came to bless my parents and me, no *yajna* was conducted, no feasts were organised, and nobody celebrated with colours, dancing in their fancy clothes.

Albeit, my parents sobbed until they were left with an emptiness inside their bodies. Neighbours grieved so many times at my birth that *Maa* once thought of killing me. *Purohits* and *pundits* accused my family of bringing a bad omen upon the village.

A newly born baby was hated by everyone in the town without doing anything to deserve that hate. His only fault was not being born up the way it was expected of him. Father and *Maa* were looked upon as culprit of a heinous crime. All because everyone was expecting from me to be a boy or a girl and as per them I was born even worse than being born as an animal. I was born a eunuch. I was born a sinner, I was born a crime.

***

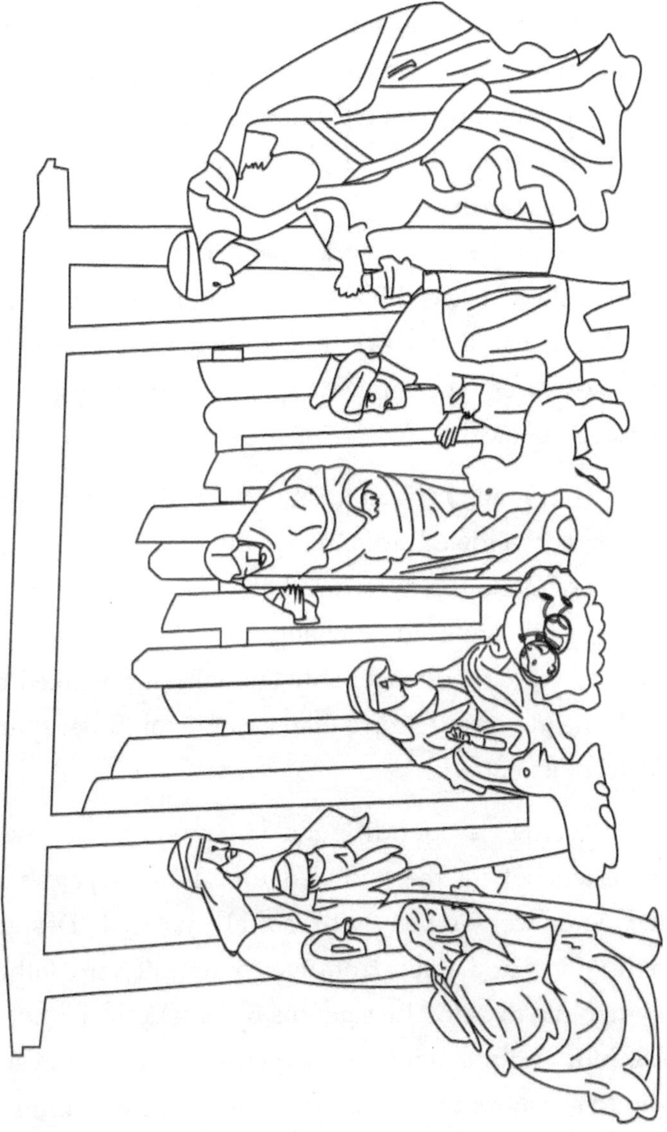

Fig. 5: Villagers abhorring the birth of Maha-Purohit.

Father was a small farmer and a respected pundit who knew much about astrology, and *Maa* taught dance and music to the women of the village. Everything seemed to be going well. Father's deeds were praiseworthy. People came to consult him before doing any auspicious work. Even if something went wrong, they asked him for the remedy. Being an astrologer, Father always tried to help everyone with the measures mentioned in the scriptures and astrology books.

But it all changed upside down after my birth. I was never allowed to attend any *Gurukul* for my formal schooling. It was not that Father did not have anything to give in exchange for my studies in *Gurukul*, he earned reasonably enough. But he liked to teach me at home, fearing that society would not spare me from its hatred.

Being a pundit and a scholar, he was enlightened with the knowledge of *Vedas, Upanishads* and was well-versed with social customs. Despite getting hate and abhor from the community, my father wanted me to help other people by becoming a scholar like him and managing my expenses from whatever I would get in return for my service to the community. I was not very fond of him doing farming in the fields from the beginning. Although I helped him from time to time, I had no interest in doing agriculture for a living.

As I grew up, hatred among people for me being a eunuch grew exponentially. I started noticing a strange change in people's behaviour. During my teenage, I realised that people didn't have the same respect even for Father as they would have when I was much younger. Some ultimately turned a blind eye to his presence in social gatherings and meetings. Few went ahead and even passed harsh and robust comments on his character and karma in the past. Or maybe, people were cunning from the beginning, it was me who couldn't notice their true colours earlier when I was a child.

With the advent of *Kali-Yuga* rising in the holy land of Kashi, inhabitants saw *pundits* as those who misguide others for their benefit. It wasn't entirely their fault as some of the *pundits* indeed did evil in the name of dharma. Half of the village had already loathed my family, partly because I was a eunuch. I had no friends to play with, no relatives to celebrate with and nobody else to talk to. Eventually, Father lost his farming land as some goons took over it. We did not want to engage in any fight against anyone. So,

Father quietly tolerated everything until he couldn't take it anymore. The wrath of *Kali-Yuga* gushed on all, but I was totally unaware of it.

One day, Father did not return home till late evening. He always came home soon after sunset. But that day, he wasn't back even after dark. Seeing *Maa* worried, I decided to go to the farm. Upon reaching, I saw him sitting under a tree and sobbing like a child. His condition made me lose my wit. I was so shocked at the sight of him crying that I didn't even ask what had happened. I took him home with me, holding his arm firmly into my hand.

***

Later that night, he told *Maa* to pack our bags and take whatever we could. He was told, somewhat threatened by those goons to leave the village permanently. Nobody wanted us to live there. We knew that other *pundits* and influencers of the village planted the seed of disgust and detestation in everybody's mind against us, but we couldn't do anything about it. *Maa* insisted on bringing up the issue in the *Panchayat*, but Father knew nothing would happen there except for our insult and abuse as the committee itself had corrupt people in it who endorsed that threat to our family.

Fig. 6: Maha-Purohit's father sitting under a tree, sobbing.

We moved to the other side of the Ganges into the capital of Rudraputra and got settled there eventually. Nobody there knew about me being a eunuch. It was not that obvious to others to know my orientation when I was younger. Changes to my body only became prominent after I entered manhood. But people would come to know about me being different sooner or later. Even if my identity was revealed, there should not be any jinx in the capital as its people were relatively developed and devoid of the general conservative mindset. Besides, there were many more like me in the capital.

People noticed Father's hard work on the farms and his service to the community. Years after our settlement in the capital town, his graceful deeds reached the kingdom of Rudraputra. We had no clue of it until the day he was called upon by the King. As time passed, he began teaching astrology and promoting the knowledge of the scriptures in the royal palace. The King often consulted him for getting astrological predictions that were deemed suitable for commencing any project in the kingdom. By the time I turned into an adult, my father had trained and educated me well in astrology and theology. I would often assist him in his work in the palace.

With each passing day, I saw the King becoming obsessed with Father's predictions and remedies. I even talked with Father about that excess confidence of the King in his predictions, but there was nothing he could do. Neither he refused the royal orders and invitations of the King, nor he had enough zeal to move away from the capital and settle down somewhere else. We had done enough escaping. All he could do was to assist the King in his projects and personal life, predicting the future to the best of his knowledge and calculations. He became a royal astrologer and *pundit*. I had a hunch that something, someday might go wrong with Father's predictions and that it would make him face King's anger and wrath. Little did I know that the day which I feared the most was about to come.

After a few days, the King asked Father if Rudraputra should sign a business deal with the kingdom of Vaishali. Father, after carefully assessing all astrological factors suggested the King sign the agreement. I don't know what went wrong with my father's calculations, but Rudraputra incurred a significantly massive loss of royal treasure after entering that deal with Vaishali. The then king of Vaishali accused Rudraputra of being fraud in the business, and our kingdom blamed Vaishali of some other double-dealing actions. The so-called good political relations between both the countries soured. The King supplanted with red bubbling anger, banished Father to a location still unknown. He couldn't afford to kill my father as he always wanted to use Father's knowledge to his benefit in the future. *Maa*, upon knowing all of this went to the palace and publicly condemned King's actions. The King, no matter how learned and wise he was, couldn't tolerate his insult and control his anger, banishing *Maa* too. Then the royal army was sent in search for me to be punished or expelled or perhaps killed, who knows, but I got lucky in escaping the capital.

I ran barefoot in a direction unknown to me and kept on walking for several days. I never met my parents after that. They are probably dead now. I cried all that day until my eyes lost all the water they had, biting my lips to prevent the outburst of emotions. It seemed as if I was being sucked up from the inside. I felt powerless, trapped in a dark void that consumed everything. There was nothing I could do to set my parents free, to put our lives back on track as it was before my birth and to reverse my haunting past. I was responsible for their misery, I was born evil, I was a curse on my family.

I wanted to go back to *Maa*'s womb, where everything was subtle. It was only after I came into this world that the fate of my family got sealed, that their lives became miserable, that the darkness prevailed all over them and remained in their lives forever after that.

My escape brought me to another village near the valley on the banks of the river. I had never visited or heard about that settlement before. One thing was for sure that I came very far from the capital. The valley was beautiful and stretched before me like a greenish-brown blanket of grass and soil. I remember climbing downhill and walking into the streets only to find nobody there. At first, I wondered if I am in Rudraputra. But then I saw the royal flag swinging on a bamboo pole near the *choupal*.

As the night would soon prevail, I randomly knocked some doors for help. The very first door that was opened for me was of Vyas's house. Seeing an exhausted eunuch on their door at that time of the day could make anyone freak out and agitated. I expected questioning and investigation from Vyas as well. But he looked welcoming and asked me to come inside, folding his hands before me in appreciation even before I could utter something. I wasn't expecting anything as respectful, rewarding and relieving as that treatment.

Vyas appeared to be losing his boyhood and becoming a man. His voice was buoyant, face covered with a moderately thick beard, indicating he could be around mid-twenties. He lived with his old mother in that house. I didn't want to tell about my past to anybody, so I made up a story and told Vyas. Being so innocent and righteous, he trusted every word that came out of my mouth that night. I wasn't interested in knowing their family history either. His mother offered me a place to sleep in their hut. I assured them I would leave early in the morning. That was my first interaction with Vyas. I had no clue that Vyas and his village would become an essential part of my personal and professional life in the future.

The next day, I commenced my journey from Vyas's house to a place even far away from the capital but still unknown to me. I wanted to reach as far as I could from the palace to save myself from the King. And as I kept on going farther away, I felt even safer. It was another neighbouring village that became my home permanently for a decade or so. That village was not inhabited entirely at that time. So, I got to settle and adjust myself there without any questions and objections raised. Nobody knew where my parents were, what my past was except that I was a eunuch. I couldn't hide my visible identity after turning into an adult, and luckily, nobody in my village had any problems with that. Eventually, I began working on the farms, something that I never wanted to do when I was a child. After getting some recognition in society, I started telling people about right and wrong as per astrology. Sometimes, I taught children some lessons from *Upanishads*, Gita and *Vedas*. I quit farming once I earned enough money and commodities in exchange for my service to the people.

In no time I was being venerated as one of the highest priests in that village. I never forgot Vyas's generosity and often visited his village which wasn't very far from mine. The second time I met Vyas after few years, he was already married to Sumati. I also got to know that Vyas's mother passed away. She died a natural death.

As I would keep coming to meet Vyas and Sumati, I developed good relations with other people in the neighbourhood, offering my service to people in Vyas's village. Slowly and steadily, I became famous for my *Jyotish* knowledge and preaching of scriptures. The more time I spent in that village, the better I got to know about Vyas's reputation. He was highly respected because of his charitable nature towards others. At times, I felt neglected by the people because of Vyas's presence and influence on them. I didn't let this feeling of insecurity prevail inside me initially. So many years had gone by so quickly that I almost forgot about my past. It didn't bother me to have escaped from the capital to save my life. Though I had some faded memories of the childhood time spent with *Maa* and Father, yet it didn't matter to me then.

Amidst being neglected and treated by the society as a less eminent person than Vyas, facing the discrimination and hatred of those people for being a eunuch and being approached by them only if they had some work, came the good news that subsided my agony up to some extent. The king of Rudraputra died of a rare disease, and his son took charge of the throne.

His son was the least competent and deserving candidate for the throne. But that is how it works, so let it be. I had seen King's son many times before while working at the palace with Father. He did not at all care about the policies and people of the kingdom. All he wanted was the money and women to have fun with. Most of the times, he was found intoxicated, lying on the roads of Rudraputra.

Alcohol and women became his greatest weakness. A few casual encounters with beautiful women of the kingdom made him fall for it. He would do anything to get them and to get drunk. His addiction was such that he would not at times care for his father's royal order. He was often caught lying, cheating and stealing for his personal benefits. It came to me as a shock when I heard he became the king of Rudraputra. I knew I would take my revenge from the kingdom for treating my parents like filth. I must end its monarchy in the future. Day and night, all I figured out was how am I going to do that. I was glad I escaped from the palace a long time ago as under the new king, the capital was not going to be as prosperous and glorified as it used to be under his father. Bitter days came as *Kali* took over the kingdom and walloped its people.

After spending a few months of winter in my village, I planned to go meet Vyas. It had been about a year since I last met him. While the primary reason for me going to another village was meeting with Vyas and Sumati, yet a compelling urge to expand my business in that village played a vital role in taking me there. I liked the recognition and respect people gave me for my seniority and service to them. I pretended as if I was doing my job as a charity but had cultivated hidden desires of earning money, respect and power. I made good money and over the time got another house built in Vyas's village. It was not as big as my first house in my town but spacious enough to accommodate a small family.

My success and rising goodwill among the people made me forget Vyas's help to me in the past. All that kept on growing was a feeling of jealousy and insecurity. I never wanted to cause any harm to Vyas and his family on a personal level. But it was my strongest desire to see him lose his influence over the community and respect that he would earn from the people. I longed to become more respected than Vyas, at any cost.

I now realise that respect is not something to be demanded, it is earned. I wish I had perceived it very early in my life. I was losing control over my thoughts for some reasons. I don't know whether it had to do something with my troubled past, my muzzled feelings and desires. I didn't know if my behaviour was a result of a psychological breakdown that was buried somewhere inside my mind and slowly affecting my thoughts and actions without me even realising. Or maybe the sudden and immense exposure to the people which I was kept deprived of in my childhood came to me as a mental shock. Whatever it was, I just knew it was not right, and yet I didn't want to do anything to make it right.

A few days later, I got an invitation from Vyas's village, requesting me to come over and bless Vyas and Sumati. I had a hunch of what might have happened and later got to know that I was right. Sumati was pregnant with her first child, wanting me to predict the nature, time and future of the baby. I was happy for them at first, but then the demon inside me spanned its wings, and I became careless suddenly. It wasn't my priority anymore to visit Vyas after getting that good news.

Anything that made Vyas happy triggered passive anger inside me and made me envy their comfortable lives. But I had to go there to maintain my helpful image and to prevent myself from becoming the topic of discussion among people by not visiting Vyas and Sumati when they really needed my help. It was for the first time Vyas had asked for my favour. I was already thinking of going there anyway. So, I went there.

Upon reaching the village, I was welcomed with great pomp as usual. That enthusiasm with which I was greeted had become mundane to me.

I expected from those villagers to greet me with the same zeal and excitement each time even though I never did anything special to deserve it. I met Vyas and Sumati and everybody else. By that time, I also became eager to know what planets and stars in the cosmos had in their astonishing forces for Vyas's child. I thought of it to be as ordinary as any other prediction that I had made in the past. How could I foresee that it would become the most exciting and complicated calculation for me, packed with a mysticism that baffled my spirit?

***

I sat on the *choupal*, surrounded by the villagers, all staring at me with an optimistic gaze as if it was me who would govern the future of the baby. As if I had the power to see the upcoming and thus, control it. I was dwelling on that false sense of authority. I began my calculations, preparing some documents required for astrological predictions. It took me a few seconds and then a few minutes afterwards to register new information and pattern of the stars. To my amazement, the calculations once ought to be ordinary became completely strange to me. I knew something divine was perpetuating in the universe ready to be showered upon the child.

I felt like someone, or something just took my knowledge and expertise in astrology, making those natal charts extremely difficult for me to understand initially.

Despite becoming anxious and worried about those charts, I maintained a decent smiling face to deflect any embarrassing moment in public. At times, I felt those people disappearing in front of me. What remained in front of my eyes were those complex natal charts and horoscope booklet, consuming all my wisdom and leaving me with nothingness to ponder upon. Vyas, Sumati and other villagers were now even more concerned about my predictions. Their presence made me conscious of doing my math.

I desired for solitude, asking Vyas to take me to his house. I was escorted by Vyas to his house, and the entire village followed me until there. Vyas and I sat inside one of the rooms, and all others waited outside the hut. I was so engulfed in my work that I could not keep track of time. It was Vyas who made me realise that I was taking a little too long that day and he asked if everything was alright. I had no answer to his question yet, so I looked at him with a thoughtful gaze and asked him to take everybody to the *choupal* and wait until I arrive there with my results.

I tried to make myself calm and imagined how Father would have calculated everything if he was to predict about the child. It was then when I came back to my senses and gradually regained the control over my faculties. I was bound to spend some more hours working and preparing my results. Once ready with the results, I left for the *choupal* where Vyas and Sumati eagerly waited with everyone else for me. I starved by that time, and to my sheer surprise, villagers had already prepared delicious food for me. I saw a feeling of relief on their faces after seeing me coming with the results. I ate my food with other *Jyotish-Acharyas* and thanked them all for bringing it for me.

Later that evening, I explained what astrology suggested about the nature, time and future of the child who would be named as Eklavya, the one who learns bow by watching. Vyas was in bliss, his eyes filled with light and mind in delight of soon becoming a father. The birth of Eklavya was going to be another hit on my pride, and I couldn't afford my self-esteem going down in front of Vyas. People would soon find another reason to mingle with Vyas and his family, and that might leave me unattended and disowned.

***

Unable to know the difference between right and wrong, virtuous and evil, I decided to kill Eklavya in Sumati's womb. Before retreating to my village, I gave some poisonous herbs to Sumati, falsely assuring the health of her newborn if she regularly consumes it. I could have stayed there until Eklvaya's birth, rather death but I didn't want to get caught for what I did to Sumati. So, I retreated to my village, keeping myself out of the scene in case something goes wrong with Sumati's labour.

Few weeks after, on the full moon day, I revisited Vyas's village. I remembered it to be the day Sumati would give birth to Eklavya. I saw Vyas going to another village to buy some seeds for agriculture. It took me by surprise to find out that Vyas didn't realise that the day of his son's birth had arrived. I could have reminded him of Eklavya's birth, but that would have made me worried about the aftermath of the unfortunate event that was going to occur in the night. I stayed in my house in Vyas's village that day, keenly waiting for the demonic night to prevail.

And when the silvery moon, perfectly round in shape gave off its brilliant light against the dark midnight sky, I sat near the window to see how things unfold. My demons, killing all my angels inside, decided to watch the show of survival that night.

Moonlight outnumbered the efforts lampposts made to spread their weak rays around them. That night could either fulfil Vyas's dream of becoming a father or become the worst nightmare of his life. After a while, Sumati opened the door of her house, coming out moaning in deep pain. She went on *Amma's* door to call for help. Even though my eyes could only see one instance at a time, I made them stride as far as they could go to see what exactly was going on at *Amma's* door. I once again tilted my head skyward, admiring the moonlight that was gloriously witnessing the melodrama with me. Seemed as if I was enjoying that tête-à-tête with that silent full-moon night. And when I looked back at the scene, I saw some women setting up a camp with some bedsheets and *sari* and Sumati was lying inside it with *Amma* and some assistants.

Few men stood a little far away from the field, waiting for Eklavya to arrive in this sinful world. I could hear at intervals the distant whimpers of Sumati trying to push the baby out. *Amma* and others calmed her agitation and anxiety down. And suddenly there was a pin drop silence all over. Sumati stopped moaning, *Amma* and other women were utterly still, and those men appeared to have become mannequins, devoid of any motion. A spooky emptiness oozed from the camp. For a moment, I felt as if what I had just seen was in my dreams only.

It was at that very moment of silence when I realised a shocking contradiction in the situation. How could I have spent a whole day calculating the birth of Eklavya going to happen on that full moon night, and predicting his future so precisely if he wasn't meant to be born with life and was going to die that night? My calculations could never go wrong. And if it was so, then what about those herbs I gave to Sumati? I wasn't ready to believe that she, after being explicitly told by me to consume it, didn't do so. At that very moment, my mind baffled with an ocean of thoughts, flickering to swat each possibility related to Eklavya's birth and death.

After that tiny window of time passed, I heard a faraway first cry of the baby that didn't belong in that time. I saw men jumping and walking towards the camp to take a closer look at the baby. They danced as if they had forgotten how to stand still, which they were a few moments ago. Had I not been born as a eunuch, people would have celebrated by birth too, dancing all night and eating feasts.

If that expected childbirth had occurred the right way, something unexpected might have happened the wrong way. *'Oh! Lord, what have I done!'* I figured out that Eklavya's birth would take Sumati's life. The herb that was supposed to harm Eklavya in the womb might cause internal bleeding, killing Sumati instead of the baby. I realised that Eklavya was destined to be born. But I never wished for Sumati's death! That unfortunate speculation left my insides cold and contracting. I felt my limbs going numb, heart exploding inside my chest. While I was recovering from the shock, my ears picked up a distant wailing. One cry supplemented with few others and gradually increased a few levels. Seemed as if *Amma* and her assistants were crying.

My fear of Sumati being dead right after Eklavya's birth had become a reality. In an instant, the moon hid behind a thick wall of black clouds. The sudden decrease in the temperature and change of weather took me by surprise. It started pouring heavily as they all crouched and gathered in the camp. The rain was a cry of nature upon the undeserved demise of a noblewoman.

Nobody saw me watching them, but I was there from the very beginning, watching all of it that was happening. I never realised when the time went by, and dawn prevailed. I clearly saw a group of people surrounding the camp, with their faces swollen, some still crying while others unable to cry anymore. It was time for me to step out of my house and act as shocked as I could look. Though I was somewhat moved by the unexpected departure of Sumati yet that dramatic event took over my feeling of sorrow. All that one could naturally see on my face was a sense of confusion and wonder.

I arrived in the field where everyone was. Many more people gathered around in a circle to see what was going on. Some of them looked at me, hoping that I would say something. But I turned down my eyes at the dead body, escaping any questions people might have for me.

Vyas arrived soon after the sunrise. *Amma* once again burst into tears, empathising with Vyas. As far as I knew Vyas, he would gather himself piece by piece and react thoughtfully. He had been meditative by temperament. But I was wrong. Vyas lost it completely, falling on the ground almost unconsciously upon the sight of his dead wife laying in front of him draped in white cloth.

He wasn't accepting his wife's sudden death, vigorously shaking Sumati's body in the hope that life would return to her.

His actions profoundly and genuinely made me stoop down in my own sight. I cursed myself for my sinful deed. Later, I assisted Vyas in performing the last rites of Sumati's dead body and retreated to my village. I deeply regretted my intentions and the results they had brought. I could never know I had a much worse role to play in the future.

~~~***~~~
~~~

Fig. 7: Maha-Purohit & Vyas looking at Sumati's pyre.

Acharya Virbhadra

My journey as a guru started on a very sudden and saddened note. Though I wanted to remain a student all my life, learning various life-lessons at different stages, yet destiny had some strange plans for me. Although my devotion to my master and his teachings was so powerful, there was no eascape from the cruelty of fate. It brought down its wrath so heavily upon us - the proponents of *Advaita Vedanta*, that we didn't get time to brace ourselves for its impact.

The sudden death of our guru, Adi Shankaracharya left Bhushan and me intensely drenched in distress for several months. Shankaracharya, after completing his spiritual tour of *Bharat-Varsha*, wanted some time to concentrate on his upcoming project of spreading the knowledge of the scriptures all over the world. He stayed with us in our Kedarnath *matha* and was planning upon opening more *Gurukul*s in the northern part of the subcontinent.

We hiked only a little far away on the Himalayan trail that passed from behind the Kedarnath temple to check the feasibility of establishing a knowledge centre there.

Up there, was a small base camp set up by other *yogis* who knew Shankaracharya from the past. We stayed there for a few days, discussing our expansion scheme with those *yogis*. It was on the last day of our stay at the camp on the Himalayas that Shankaracharya postponed his plan of coming down to the *matha* near Kedarnath temple. At first, Bhushan and I thought it to be his wish to stay there for long. But soon we realised it was something else that bothered him.

By the evening of that day, his health deteriorated quickly. He spent his day laying numb on the mat. He would not take any medications either and asked us to leave him alone for some time whenever we tried convincing him of seeking medical aid. Bhushan was worried about him, so was I and everybody else in the camp.

Shankaracharya never had any health problems before, not any that we were aware of. We had known him for about fifteen years. He trained his body to walk barefoot in soil, snow, mud, rock and whatnot. He could sit in the sun, rain, wind and cold for prolonged durations. Shankaracharya trained his mind well enough to achieve what an average human could never think of. Then what took his life at an early age of thirty-two? – this question still baffles my mind.

Some *yogis* prepared dinner in the kitchen while Bhushan and I sat in another hall, creating lessons for our students in Kedarnath *matha*. I heard *Acharya* calling Bhushan, laying on his mat and upon our arrival, asked both of us to bring every other *yogi* in his room. I hunched *Acharya* was going to give up his life, but he indeed was sure of departing from this world that very evening. All the *yogis* in the camp gathered around *Acharya*, some offering to help him get up and sit on his yoga mat only to get his refusal – he sat all by himself, thanking *yogis* for their hospitality, further advising them not to cook his dinner for that night and instructed Bhushan and me to go to an old and remotely established *Gurukul* atop a mountain in the state of Rudraputra and give our service there.

That *Gurukul* was a joint venture of *Acharya* Sivaguru, Adi Shankaracharya and some local *yogis* that shared same principles. Shankaracharya specifically hinted us about our role in shaping up the future of Rudraputra but never told us what exactly was going to happen, how Bhushan and I serving to a *Gurukul* on an isolated mountain peak was going to change the fate of Rudraputra, a kingdom that seemed all flourishing in glory already. I tried asking him the reason behind sending us both there, but he purposely ignored my question, giving us a riddle to solve - something that he never did in the past. He said,

"You don't go seek the change, the change to the fate of Rudraputra will come to you all by itself; all you have to do is to wait for it and welcome it with both of your hands wide open once it reaches there. A poor farmer, destined to hardships but best of the best people in Rudraputra will reach out to you seeking your help, make sure you wisely do whatever you can to help him. The rest shall happen on its own."

Seemed like he knew about the future unfolding of the events that when revealed before time, could destroy its essence. *Acharya* then told us about the ending of his life as he sat in *padmasana,* folding his both hands in gratitude and gently closed his eyes. We all looked at him for a few seconds and realised he was not breathing – his chest wouldn't rise and fall as before. The moment I touched his feet firmly to give him a nudge, his cold body fell on the floor. He was no more, and with his demise, prevailed sorrow all over the base.

Fig. 8: Shankaracharya in padmasana, preparing for his departure to final abode.

Though I, being a *yogi* mastered the art of keeping my mind calm in the wildest of the situations, yet that death made me feel a prolonged tinge of misery which still has its footprints engraved in my mind. Bhushan cried in despair, so did all of us. Death, no matter how distinct it was, always brought sadness, and that one brought grief in abundance.

Acharya's dead body - as vibrant as before when it had life in it, was brought down to the Kedarnath *matha* in the morning. A swarm of people attended his cremation the next day. His followers, colleagues, students, and whoever wanted to pay their tribute came from all over the subcontinent. Teaching and all other administrative tasks suspended for about a week in the *matha*.

When the order restored itself in the region, Bhushan and I were all set to embark on our journey to reach the mountain-*Gurukul* of Rudraputra. We handed over our responsibilities to the remaining staff and walked eastbound along the shore of the Ganges towards our new home. A few weeks, some minor injuries, and few unexpected wildlife encounters after, we entered inside the boundaries of Rudraputra one evening.

***

Rudraputra was a scenic highland, bounded by the Ganges on one side and Samrakuta mountain range on another. In the middle sat a plateau which the fancy royal palace was located on. A combination of jungles and some villages in between guarded the plateau. Our *Gurukul* was built on the peak of a Samrakuta-mountain, devoid of any regular venturing of people and thus excluded itself from any disturbance from the rest of the world.

As Bhushan and I furthered towards the mountain-*Gurukul*, we passed through some settlements that had more people than our region at Kedarnath. That hustle and bustle in those villages never halted, bringing glory to their civic life. As we arrived late in the evening in that village near the mountain on which our *Gurukul* was built, we looked for a shelter to spend the night. Luckily, we got one gentleman who offered a room to both of us in his clay house. We were glad we arrived in that village right on time as there was only one chariot service that carried passengers uphill, and the same chariot brought others down the hill. Bhushan thought even if we miss one service, we can always get another one the next day. It was then when our host in the village told us about the service that resumed once every three months.

Bhushan must have thanked almighty for the umpteenth time that night as none of us wanted to spend any more time elsewhere but in the *Gurukul* to which we were sent by our master.

Next day early in the morning, Bhushan and I left for the peak of the mountain. Gandharv, the charioteer - as young and energetic as his horses tied with the cart, was the only one who operated that service for the *Gurukul,* as no other villager risked their horses and chariots to serve a school situated at the peak.

As our chariot climbed up the steep path, we felt our weight pulling us downward. Both the horses, despite using all the force they got, could only drag the cart with snail's pace. Bhushan looked at me with mischief in his eyes and said,

"Virbhadra, I think you will do a better job at pulling this cart up than these horses." He never missed an opportunity since our childhood days to crack jokes on my muscular built and strength.

"I will give it a shot only if you get off and walk until we reach up top," I replied to him in an instant, and both of us laughed like anything. Gandharv heard our conversation, and he laughed along.

Bhushan and I were old friends from the same village, we went to the same school and later, after meeting with *Acharya* Shankar got jobs at the same *matha*. Shankaracharya while touring the country once came to our village long ago. That day changed both of our lives for the greater good, I now realise.

Bhushan was good at studies and theology, whereas I was more interested in combat studies and martial arts. Bhushan was not as physically strong as I was, but his knowledge and ideas were way mightier than anyone else of his age. And because he was so influential and mystic in his own way, he never really needed to become physically tough to get things done efficiently. We both always got along with each other and formed a great partnership at tasks. Perhaps, that is the reason why Shankaracharya offered a job to both of us at the same Kedarnath-*matha*.

Through swivelled path that was narrow in the rocky passes and wider in between, our chariot ascended the mountain. I saw a glimpse of entire Rudraputra, the Ganges and the royal palace from inside the chariot while climbing up.

***

Fig. 9: Gandharv's chariot carrying Virbhadra & Bhushan to the Mountain-Gurukul.

The sun had finally risen, cascading down through patches of white clouds and lighting up the region. Washermen made their way to the shore of the river, farmers worked with their tools in the farms, women reared their cattle, their clothes shined bright in the morning sun. I saw it all down there from the mountain, tiny people moved even slower than our chariot.

A while after, I saw the *Gurukul*, standing atop at the peak built with a unique design. We were still a little far away from reaching it.

Gurukul was a high-rise already situated high enough to put the clouds to shame. It was designed and built by the then king of Rudraputra to be used as a watch-tower but was later given to some monks as an act of superficial charity by the king. As soon as the royal army realised that the mountain itself was the ultimate protection of the kingdom from that side, making it impossible for anyone to climb up that high from the other side of it, they abandoned the building and gave it to *Acharya* Sivaguru and his disciples.

Adi Shankaracharya often visited that *Gurukul* long ago to make sure everything was being run smoothly. And since then the *Gurukul* became home to countless students, acclaimed saints and skilled teachers and now us too. As we came closer to it, I saw its big dark windows that stared at us like a many-eyed serpent. Sunlight lit up its half, leaving the other mammoth-half wholly submerged in its own giant shadow.

Three flag-poles bearing the kingdom's seal, '*Aum*', and Shankaracharya's sketch - in that order, sentinelled *Gurukul*'s authenticity, integrity and legacy that I am proud of.

Before I could fill my eyes with more of that mesmerising view of the *Gurukul*, Gandharv stopped his chariot, informing us about the end of our trip uphill. Bhushan got off from the cart, and I followed him. We both thanked Gandharv for his service, gave him a few clothes that we got as farewell gift from our colleagues at Kedarnath-*matha* and walked towards the *Gurukul*.

Meanwhile, some passengers going downhill sat in the chariot with their luggage. We walked past the tall rusty iron gate that was opened on the one side, its other side was hinged to the stone walls. But the opening was so broad that anything as colossal as our chariot could pass through it easily. I wondered what that gate was built there years ago for, as nobody could come to the peak anyway, and what could one steal from that old building made up of rock and metal.

As Bhushan walked ahead, he cautioned me of the wet path which was damp with morning dew. A little ahead, we saw a garland of beautiful flowers, spreading their soft scent in the fresh morning air. *Gurukul* was just elegant. I knew that once in, students were only allowed to visit their family after successfully completing the three years of their initial education. If I were to study in that *Gurukul*, I would have gone home after finishing my entire education and training there. *'Who would ever want to leave such a serene place?'* I wondered while Bhushan led me to the main entrance of the building.

We passed through the hallway that goes to the main chamber where we expected to meet with Kaushalacharya, the headmaster of the *Gurukul*. We met him once before at a spiritual congression in Kashi, and he was already aware of our arrival at the *Gurukul*. Kaushalacharya was older than all the *acharya*s in the *Gurukul*. He was the disciple of Shankaracharya's father, *Acharya* Sivaguru and hailed from a southern part of the subcontinent. *Acharya* Sivaguru, before embarking on his journey to the final abode assigned Kaushalacharya with the responsibility of looking after and managing that mountain-*Gurukul*. And without a doubt, Kaushalacharya managed and took great care of the *Gurukul* and its inhabitants.

The hallway we walked through was built in between the classrooms that had few children in each one of them and *acharyas* teaching them the basics of theology. Some halls had adult students learning advanced lessons from the scriptures. While I didn't fully understand the partially heard sentences that the teachers discussed in those classrooms, Bhushan passed a smile, indicating that he knew exactly what was being taught in those classes. As we passed each hall, students gazed at us with questionable eyes and wonder. Some *acharyas* greeted us with their gestures at the very sight of us both.

That wide but enclosed hallway crowned with the noise of conversations happening inside the rooms, our footsteps and other sounds. Whatever Bhushan told me on our way to the chamber perfectly echoed several times. A little ahead was a pathway that led to the prayer and training ground. Further ahead was the kitchen and dining area where students and teachers ate their meals.

We took a few turns with the hallway, hoping to arrive at the chamber quickly, but were left disappointed every time. No wonder that building was large and spanned from one point of the peak to another. Before I lost my patience and was about to tell Bhushan to walk swiftly, we saw the main chamber. A wave of contentment ran inside my heart. We entered the room and saw Kaushalacharya sitting on his mat, doing some paperwork. As soon as he heard our footsteps, he stood up and greeted Bhushan and me respectively. Everything in the chamber was entirely in order, peace prevailed there, making me rethink what I just saw and heard in the classrooms – complete chaos.

Kaushalacharya was a bold short man with a bald head, coloured mark of sandalwood paste glorified his forehead, dry eyes that proved his decades-long service to the community and immense knowledge that he gained after mastering holy scriptures, *Upanishads* and *Vedas*. He would have made a perfect example of the mindful sage only if he had control over his short temperament.

While I never saw him losing his calm, there were talks of his anger across all the *mathas*. I knew Bhushan and Kaushalacharya would get along very well with each other. By that time, I saw some more *acharyas* and *Gurukul* staff with their head completely shaved.

Finding myself the only one to have long matted hair like Shiva, as they called it, I became a little conscious. I hoped Kaushalacharya does not pass any comment on my hair, which luckily, he didn't. Both Bhushan and I knew that even if Kaushalacharya made a sarcastic comment about my hair, I would not have gotten rid of it. I never shaved my head, and I was never going to do that. Shankaracharya never asked me to shave my head. Perhaps, he knew it was something undesired to me from the very beginning.

Bhushan and I discussed with Kaushalacharya about how things were in Kedarnath after the demise of Shankaracharya. Kaushalacharya very well empathised with our situation there, relating to the times when he was left alone after his guru and Shankaracharya's father, *Acharya* Sivaguru died.

We made some plans about administering the *Gurukul* efficiently, requesting Kaushalacharya to hand us over the charge of training and teaching students. Kaushalacharya knew Bhushan was excellent in theology, philosophy and general principles of *Vedanta*, so he assigned him to the teaching to students for the initial three years and asked me if I was interested in taking up the martial arts training and combat studies for those children for three years.

Offering me to teach combat was like giving the fire its fuel, it was like asking someone utterly hungry if they want to eat or not. There was no way I could have not accepted that offer. It was then decided that students would learn theory during the day and practice combat during the evening. That routine of studying philosophy during the day and practising martial arts in the evening continued since then and is followed even now.

***

Days turned into months and months into years, countless students came in, and many went out of the *Gurukul* after completing or leaving their studies. They all came in as children – vulnerable and weak and went out as adults – wise and powerful. Bhushan and I, along with everyone else, put our sweat and blood to cultivate an empowered generation of youth, hoping that one day they will eliminate the *Kali*, but nothing happened.

Sands of time turned - Bhushan became older, Kaushalacharya even older. Seemed like it was only me in the *Gurukul* who hadn't changed from the outside, as Bhushan and others often complimented my youthful looks.

How could anybody have known that from the inside, I had gone through a drastic change? I lost my hope in life. I never wanted to be contained inside a beautiful place atop a mountain and follow a mundane lifestyle.

The scenic beauty of *Gurukul* that enchanted me with its glory for several years had finally become ordinary to me. Though I enjoyed training the students, yet I was not able to bring that change I wished for. Students came and went just like that, engulfing themselves into the same domestic lifestyle they were in before coming to *Gurukul*. Since ages, I waited for that right time to come when Bhushan and I would change the fate of the state as predicted by Shankaracharya right before his soul left his body. His predictions could never go wrong, they were all certain in the past, they will all be right in the future too. Now all I did was eagerly waiting for that time to come when I would realise my ultimate purpose and Shankaracharya's secret reason behind sending Bhushan and me from Kedarnath to Rudraputra.

For all those years, I looked for someone poor, laden with bad luck to come to us and seek help, but no one ever came to the *Gurukul*.

At times, I even doubted my master's words as to be something he just uttered under the influence of his bad health.

I wished I could time travel into past and buy Shankaracharya some more time so that he could tell me about what he knew, or maybe I could just travel into my future and see what was about to happen there and then be ready for that. I had always believed present is what shapes the future but those were the days when the future was all I thought about. It never occurred to me before, that I had stopped caring about my present and worried about the future all the time. One can and must control their actions in the present to get hold of the events of the future.

***

Days became long and nights even longer. While Bhushan attained cosmic peace through his wisdom and knowledge of scriptures, I struggled to keep uncomplainingly waiting for something that was about to change all our lives - that something was bound to create history by changing the course of time and destiny of Rudraputra. My days slipped through my fingers as I watched them passing by, standing across the empty horizon of the chaotic world inside me.

I could've trained my students better in those days, I could've done something for my colleagues, for the *Gurukul*, for Bhushan and even for myself but I was just not interested anymore in continuing what I did there for decades until one day when a letter arrived in the *Gurukul*.

That letter was sent to us through Gandharv just as all other messages were sent. It was sheer coincidence, or perhaps the set play of time that Kaushalacharya handed over that envelope to me and asked me to see what was inside it as he was occupied with some other office work. That letter seemed as ordinary as hundreds of letters we received in the *Gurukul*. It was only after I opened it I realised it was not just a letter, albeit it was the purpose of my life that I was eagerly and relentlessly waiting for! It was the path to the change that Adi Shankaracharya hinted about.

Just when I lost all my faith and hope in life, destiny restored it into me, and this time with even more enthusiasm and devotion to my work. I showed that letter to Bhushan, and his eyes sparkled with a ray of hope. We then realised we didn't have to expect someone in person to reach out to us. Both Bhushan and I remembered our guru, Shankaracharya, recalling the riddle he told us on the last day of his life. While Kaushalacharya wondered why both of us looked shockingly mesmerised after reading that letter, Bhushan and I danced as if our legs forgot to stand still. The letter was sent to us by that poor farmer that Shankaracharya had told us about years ago, on the day he departed from this world. The note read,

'Greetings! Acharya,

I am writing this letter as a poor farmer who is destined to misfortunes, a widower and a father of a thirteen-year-old boy from a small village of Rudraputra, bearing great hope in my heart that you will remember and consider my humble request after finish reading it. I lost my wife thirteen years ago to a tragic incident, as she died soon after giving birth to my child due to severe internal bleeding. Despite being bereaved of motherly love and care, my son Eklavya got all that I, his father, could give. After home-schooling him for the past several years with his grandmother, and after saving some money for the tuition, I believe I am now ready to send him for his formal education in the Gurukul. Eklavya has a great interest in learning lessons from scriptures and shows enthusiasm towards combat skills, and so this mountain-Gurukul would be the best place for him to learn and grow into a wise adult.

I could never attend any Gurukul, and so it is my only wish to see my son learning there. My parents never thought that they or I would be forgotten and lost in the world in the absence of knowledge. But they were wrong, and I don't want to commit that same mistake with my son of being ignorant and underestimating the power of education. I want Eklavya to change the way this world is, I want him to put an end to the wrath of Kali, I want my son to fight for the righteous, to bring a revolution to put an end to the suffering and anarchy in the state. Prophecies were made that he holds power to change the world. I don't know if that change will ever happen, but one thing that I know is that it would never happen on its own. Eklavya needs you, he needs your help, Acharya! Help him shape the future of Rudraputra, help him serve humanity.

Sincerely,

Vyas'

It was written on a cheap paper and in rough handwriting but bore a message that was priceless and powerful. Bhushan and I told Kaushalacharya everything about the significance of that letter sent to us by Vyas. Kaushalacharya, after listening to the riddle of Shankaracharya, testified that it was the same help that Shankaracharya talked about in his puzzle. He also agreed that if he were to read that letter first, he would have ignored Vyas' request as the *Gurukul* never accepted admission requests via letters. As a result, neither Bhushan nor I would have gotten to know about such message ever. What a shocking coincidence it was!

Parents always came there in-person to pay the fee or anything they wished to donate, and students took their admission test in the main chamber of the *Gurukul*, usually. Everything made perfect sense - Vyas reaching out to us for our help to teach and train his son that would later turn the cycle of time in Rudraputra, his misfortunate past, me getting to open and read that letter first instead of Kaushalacharya, and everything else Shankaracharya told us in his riddle, all of it was perfectly aligned.

Bhushan and I requested Kaushalacharya to get Eklavya admitted in the *Gurukul* without wasting his trip to come there to take his test first. As Eklavya was meant to pass all the trials and to bring the change in the kingdom, we bypassed doing his admission formalities. Kaushalacharya being aware of the prediction made by Adi Shankaracharya, allowed us to invite him to join the *Gurukul*. Without further due, Bhushan prepared an invitation addressing Vyas and kept it with him to hand it over to Gandharv when he visits the *Gurukul* next time after three months. Meanwhile, Kaushalacharya and I prepared results of the admission test handed over to us by the new batch of students seeking admission in the *Gurukul*.

***

Time flew by in a blink of an eye. The same days and night that stood still when I desperately waited for someone to come to us before I got that letter, now disappeared like the rabbit of the magician's hat. Those three months passed way quicker than I realised, and the day arrived when Gandharv brought few newly admitted students in the *Gurukul*. Kaushalacharya swamped and snowed under the load of paperwork, and other official responsibilities of the *Gurukul* seemed to have forgotten about Eklavya arriving in that batch, but Bhushan and I remembered, and we were excited to see the mystic child that would do wonders.

The chariot arrived little after sunrise, and disembarked few children from it, carrying their bags filled with clothes, food items and whatever their family members gave as souvenirs. Some were younger, others a little older, but they all had an innocence and a tinge of wonder on their faces.

While the sun, the wind and the birds that morning extolled the *Gurukul,* some of those kids looked sad and low on energy. Perhaps they missed their parents, relatives, they longed for their neighbours, their comfortable bed, delicious food prepared by their mothers back home. Or the fact that they will only be able to visit their homes after three years of successful completion of their studies haunted them. Whereas there were some, who were excited to see the building, the mountaintop, other children and *acharya*s. They were so enthralled by the hiking adventure that they overlooked the reality of separation and isolation from their loved ones, the truth that would soon hit them and take away their excitement from them. Kids were kids after all!

Amidst that batch was a boy walking towards where Bhushan and I stood. He was too big to be a kid but still very young with a balance of both excitement and concern visible on his face. His eyes searched for something, someone familiar but were unable to do so. Subtle walk with his head held high, a little curiosity on his face and seriousness on the forehead, reflecting his not so happy childhood that we speculated soon after getting that letter from Vyas.

Bhushan and I looked at each other, confirming that he was Eklavya, the boy we eagerly waited to see, the warrior that was destined to meet with us.

Besides him, walked another same-aged boy, a little taller than Eklavya. He came fully prepared for his hiking adventure with a wooden stick like a crutch, a water pot, a knife hanging around his waist and warrior instinct evident on his face. Seemed as if he came for a jungle safari and not to *Gurukul*. It was not his fault as that *Gurukul* being situated on the top of a mountain peak often made people concerned about the wild encounters with animals during their trek. That boy was Pundir, hailing from a village on the other side of the Ganges and the plateau, but in Rudraputra.

Bhushan and I saw our childhood days in those two. Bhushan was more like Eklavya, always curious to know things and serious in nature. While I was like Pundir, agile and always prepared for anything undesired. Seeing them walking together implied that they made good friends of each other during their journey to the mountaintop. Or they knew each other from even before that, I wasn't sure.

Fig. 10: Pundir & Eklavya walking in Gurukul's campus.

It took a while for both to settle in an entirely new environment, but they adapted well to the serene *Gurukul* as time passed. *Gurukul's* grand building and long poles with flags often enticed Eklavya to stare at them for some time whenever he could.

Bhushan taught them the art of self-control and the importance of dharma in the first year, while I trained them in archery. Eklavya defeated Pundir in the archery test and got promoted to the second year. Pundir, after taking a retest, also got pushed to the second year of studies. Eklavya was unbeatable in archery among all the students. His name itself signified his talent - the one who learns bow by watching, and he quickly learned not only archery but all combat skills that I taught him. Both of them developed similar interests in studies, but Pundir was more curious to learn all fighting skills from the beginning. He would learn only combat from me and not theory subjects, only if he could.

Though students and *acharya*s often appreciated Eklavya's hard work in theology and combat, Kaushalacharya always tried to test his skills whenever he got a chance. Bhushan and I never knew his real intentions behind doing that.

But we always assumed good faith and took it as his way of making Eklavya a better philosopher and warrior.

The second year of *Gurukul* made Eklavya even better in theology, archery and mixed martial arts. Bhushan and I really enjoyed teaching Eklavya, and sometimes Pundir too. Eklavya showed traits of becoming a warrior-leader, a wise and powerful one. After all, he was bound to change the fate of Rudraputra. But I always wondered how.

After spending three years in the *Gurukul* and passing his exams in theology and combat, Eklavya had the most robust spiritual debate of his life with Kaushalacharya. It was only after he took his test with Kaushalacharya that he could visit his family before he comes back to *Gurukul* to resume his education. Excelling that debate earned him the only headband in the *Gurukul* for students who excelled in theology, and that too in mere three years. Both Pundir and Eklavya left for their villages the next morning, but only Pundir came back. Nobody knew why Eklavya didn't.

Had I known earlier that we will lose Eklavya I would have not let him go that day. Both Bhushan and I were unsure about the training and education we gave him.

I wasn't sure if those three years of practice had made him such wise and capable of turning the future of Rudraputra, as told to us by Adi Shankaracharya. I sent few letters to Vyas through Gandharv but never got any reply from him. Even Gandharv never saw Eklavya and Vyas in their village after that. Unable to do anything else to bring Eklavya back, Bhushan and I wondered what might have happened to them. We were worried if something fatal happened to them. If it were known to me that I would train Eklavya for only three years, I would have paid more attention to his training, I would have spent more time with him, I would have given him everything that he deserved. Only if I knew I had just three years with him.

****

Once again, unrest prevailed in my mind, and this time Bhushan's too. Was that it? Was that the secret reason of Shankaracharya behind sending us there – to teach a child for three years? Was that we both were destined to do? Would those three years of training and education make Eklavya someone who could eliminate *Kali*? Why only we were sent to train him? Was that the part Bhushan and I were to play in this game of karma and kismet?

Several of such unsolved mysteries distracted us for few months, but then we regained control of our faculties, bringing our body and mind back to teaching students.

I tried my best after that not to think about Eklavya and whatever strange I had gone through but could never do away with it entirely. The cycle of time changed, and I evolved with it accordingly, hoping that someday I would get to see my favourite student, Eklavya.

~~~***~~~
~~~

Fig. 11: Acharya Virbhadra, thoughtful about the future of Rudraputra & Eklavya.

Eklavya

It had been a few days since I walked and still hadn't crossed Rudraputra yet. Neither I knew what direction I initially headed to – I kept on walking in the course of the mountains. It was for the first time in eight years of my rule that I toured my state mostly on foot. Unlike handful who saw me from close enough in the past, most of the inhabitants of Rudraputra did not recognise me as their king. Probably, because I was all by myself in simple *yogic* attire and with my head shaved, holding a wooden stick that primarily served as a crutch while on long walking journeys.

I used to wear regal clothes, had long hair and was always seen in the public surrounded by the royal guards and often with *Maha-Purohit* on my political tours. But none of that would help me on the spiritual voyage I was about to begin. So, I left all of it in the palace. What remained with me was my body, mind and soul.

I walked during most of the day, taking some rests in between the treks and sought shelter at night. I spent many nights in the jungle and several in the villages that I passed through.

Fig. 12: One of the nights when Eklavya slept in the jungle.

People generally allowed me to stay with them in their houses. As I had no money on me, I obtained food by asking for alms. Those who gave me food, shelter and clothes learned one or two lessons of *Upanishads* and Bhagwat Gita in return. All thanks to *Acharya* Bhushan for giving me the extensive knowledge of scriptures.

There were times when I stayed for longer durations in the villages due to the humble requests of local people as some of them recognised me as their king. I would then inform them about my contemporary renunciation from the kingship of Rudraputra and that Bibhatsu headed the kingdom in my absence. I would teach the entire community about *Vedanta* and its philosophies. Sometimes, I even showed them some self-defence techniques of martial arts.

*****

Few weeks passed following the same lifestyle. I got to know I was heading towards the kingdom of Vaishali. I could see their land from where I was staying. After spending a few days in the town that was on the outskirts of Rudraputra, I conveyed my host the urge to continue my spiritual journey. Everybody in the neighbourhood bid me farewell, giving me food and some clothes to be utilised in the future. I commenced my walk from that town to the last village on our border before I would enter Vaishali. I wanted to halt in that village, reaching there by the evening that day as I had seen the consequence of knocking the doors after dusk, very well remembering what happened to Tara and me in that village where bandits attacked. Nobody helped the wounded us, deeming we would pose a threat to them. They weren't wrong. Anyways, I could not even tell the people of the border village that I am their king as who would have believed a monk-looking intruder to be the king of one of the mightiest kingdoms in the region.

The village was situated on the far side of the Ganges. After walking continuously for more than half of the day, I eagerly wanted to sit somewhere and eat my food given to me by my host in the former town. But finding a suitable place to relax and munch was not easy in that dense jungle.

The jungle had already thumped up all my senses badly, leaving me utterly exhausted. Moreover, it reminded me of the fight for survival that Tara and I had with the bear about a decade ago. The situation was different now. I did not, at all, fear any attack by any wild animal there.

My sleek wooden crutch was enough of a weapon for me to use in any combat for that matter. Probably, because I was very well trained to protect myself. *Acharya* Virbhadra made me a better and confident warrior. But I felt too tight in the jungle. There came a point when the chirping of the birds, the sound of the crickets, and larger animals banged inside my head, resulting in a headache. It all seemed to be the natural symphony at the beginning that soothed my mind. The only thing that had kept me going until then was the fresh air that tasted like mint and lavender. I was blocked by the bushes, branches and shrubberies scattered in every direction.

At times, I was completely unaware of the direction I was heading towards. I struggled for a while, making my way through that dense part of the forest. A little ahead, there was an open space that seemed perfect for me to have my meal and take rest for a while. Banana leaves fallen from the porous trunks made an ideal bedsheet for me to sit and lay upon.

As soon as I opened my nicely packed meal bag, a whiff of the food entered my nose, producing more saliva in my mouth than ever. Had that smell came out of the sac earlier, I would not have kept my food for so long. I knew I was going to eat my food as if it was going to be my last meal. I had soft bread drenched with some butter, an apple, and vegetable curry in the bag. I could have eaten the entire apple at once, only if I could have opened my mouth any wider. I made much noise while eating, feeling no embarrassment for behaving like a kid. Within few minutes, I consumed that delicious food which took who knows how many hours to cook. After that, I cleaned up my lips with a cloth and drank some water. I was so full that I couldn't drink any more water to satisfy my thirst. I realised I did not even chew the food adequately and quickly gulped it without even pausing to breathe.

After relaxing and taking a quick nap under a tree, I resumed my walk to the village at the border. As far as my calculations were concerned, I could tell that I was not very far from reaching my destination.

After walking for some time, I felt a sudden decrease in temperature. At first, I thought it was because of the sunset, but then I saw the patches of bright sunlight penetrating through the scattered spots between the dense leafy branches of the sky-scraping deodar and banyan trees. It was now confirmed that the sun was still in the sky, probably a little bit far from the western horizon. *'Then what can cause this sudden coolness in the air?'* I wondered inside my head while continuing my walk. The cluttering sound of water entered my ears, pointing my thoughts towards the only possibility of a river in the jungle. *'The Ganga!'*, my mind answered in anxiety. How could I forget about the mighty river that spanned in between the forest and the border?

As I walked closer to the end of the jungle, the breeze became colder. I heard the flowing water much clearly that had a hypnotic quality. Suddenly, a rush of blood ran inside my body, making me realise that I had to swim through the stream to get to the shore as there might not be any boatmen in that area. Even though there might be someone to help, I did not have any money or anything for that matter to offer them. I could have swum through the river quite comfortably, but the stream was stronger there, as far as the sound suggested. I was yet far from the edge of the jungle to be able to see the situation there.

Meanwhile, my mind prepared the plan to cross the river. *'Someone would have made arrangements for me to cross the river easily, had I been in the palace,'* I thought while smirking at the challenge that I would soon face. *'What would I do if there is really no boatman on this side of the shore?'* I was a little worried and then simultaneously turned around, running as fast as I could to reach the spot where I had seen a scattered bunch of banana trees. I was thinking of carrying one trunk of the banana tree and use it as a natural floater. It could at least keep me from drowning in the current.

***

Upon reaching there, I found few semi-rotten trunks already detached from the ground. They were not in the condition I expected yet good enough to carry my weight in the water. I put one log on my shoulder and proceeded with pace towards the river. Upon reaching to the edge of the jungle, I saw the swirls appearing and vanishing on the surface of the Ganga. The river always kept on flowing towards its destiny no matter what. Sun rays reflecting from its surface made the water look like a massive plain of sparkling diamonds.

Though the bag and everything inside it was going to be wet, yet it was of great use to me. It had some clothes that I got from the villagers and previous hosts as almsgiving. I tied the string of the bag tightly to the banana trunk, making sure it would not float away in the river. The raging water of Ganga took me to my childhood several years back, reminding me of the day I took the plunge in it to collect some coins to buy my food. It was the day when I left my village, swam through the river to get across the other side of it, took a deep plunge in it to collect some coins that tourists and commuters threw in it to make a wish and was about to end my life in the river that same day. It was the day Mohammad saved my life.

Lost in those memories, I felt intense goosebumps. I put all my weight on the front of my feet, filling as much air I could load into my lungs and jumped off the cliff holding the trunk tightly. My mind was blank in those few moments of my flight, body fully prepared to sustain the temperature shock that the cold water of the Ganges was about to give me. Seconds after, I was in the river, flowing with its current that would take me to the shore. The water appeared to be calm almost immediately after getting into the river. Soon, I realised it was me who was swept away to a far distance by the water and not the river that turned calm. The spot where I jumped off from the cliff still ruffled the valley.

***

I appreciated my decision of taking that trunk with me. I would have struggled a lot in the water without it. While holding on to the banana trunk in the river, I saw several pathways to my own village where I was born, where I played with my friends, and where I used to be treated like family. I hadn't forgotten that it was the same place where I was banished from, the same land that declared me cursed. I hadn't forgotten my past and childhood spent with *Amma* and Father, yet it was too late to walk down the immersive memory lane. I had come a long way, leaving behind the painful past and all the evil I had gone through.

The moment I was about to get my hands off that trunk, I discovered my bag was not tied to it anymore. The mighty force of the water took the bag with it who knows where. A wave of disappointment ran inside my heart. Suddenly, I realised I had left my crutch on the cliff. I did not even remember if I had left it on the cliff or at the place where I ate my food in the jungle. But it didn't matter.

I let the trunk go in the direction where the flow took it and started swimming to the shore. The water was calm there, and I could see some ferries commuting along the river. After a while, I reached the bank of the river. I felt a sudden increase in my body weight, walking out of the river in my wet clothes. I had arrived in the last village of my kingdom on the Rudraputra - Vaishali border in time. A smile appeared on my face, seeing the sun was not fully set yet.

I kept on walking until I crossed the outskirts and reached the village. On my way walking towards the main *choupal* in the village, I passed many grocery stalls with their counters full of fruits and vegetables, and many small shops selling clothes, utensils and household stuff. I walked through a nursery that displayed flowers, shrubberies and a specific kind of crop. It appeared to be wheat but of some different quality that I had never seen before in the capital or anywhere else.

As the dusk prevailed, there were fewer people on the road and very few bullock carts and cattle. Villagers, mostly men, gathered around the *choupal* to meet and greet each other every evening. It was also commonplace to hold meetings and hearings regarding local disputes. I hoped to see the head of the village there so that I could ask for a place to spend my night. As I approached near the *choupal*, I saw a few elderly men sitting around it. Some played cards, others were discussing something, while few were just relaxing under the tree. I asked if anyone among those men was the head of the village, folding my hands and greeting them. The head was not there, but I was given the directions to his house. Nobody among them recognised me as the king of Rudraputra. I was glad not to reveal and explain my identity.

'Probably the head of the village does not know anything about me either', I wondered. The remote location of that village from the capital might be one of the reasons why people were less likely to recognise me as their king. I walked towards the suggested way to reach head's house. My clothes were almost dry now.

The sun had finally set in the sky, leaving behind the scarlet horizon that still emitted some light. I arrived outside the house. It was a clay hut that seemed to be a timid rabbit surrounded by giant trees all around it. Few branches twisted over its roof as if they were claiming their right over the hut. I knocked on the thin wooden door that was slightly opened. My mind expected some strange reaction from the person who would see me standing at their door. I had already prepared in my mind the things that I had to say to the head of the village.

***

Fig. 13: Evening gathering of elderly men at Choupal.

I was about to knock on the door for the second time, but I heard someone coming closer to it from the inside. The footsteps were steady and slow, implying either the person was lazy to go to the door or they must be old. While I made these speculations about the village-head in my mind, the door opened. I saw an elderly person standing, with his eyes struggling to remember my face. Whereas, I was stunned and surprised at the very sight of him. He was none other than the *Sarpanch Ji*. The person who came to meet me in my capital, the man whom my father knew very well. *Sarpanch Ji* kept my father in his house the night before my birth, and there I stood right outside that house in front of the same person.

"*Sarpanch Ji*, hope you remember me. I am Eklavya, you came to meet me in my palace almost a decade ago." I tried to remind him of our meeting.

"Oh, I have become older but haven't lost my memory yet. Of course, I remember you Eklavya." He smiled and asked me to come inside.

"You look so different now. What have you done to your head?" he laughed, pointing out to my clean-shaven skull, hugging me gently with his weak arms.

"Nothing, it was difficult to maintain long hair, so I just got rid of it," I replied.

Sarpanch Ji staunchly followed *Brahmacharya*, so he had no family and lived by himself in that small hut with an open-air veranda. After eating our dinner together, he made two beddings on the veranda for us to sleep.

While we ate our food, he bombarded a series of questions on me, asking about all that had happened in the last decade after he left the palace. He was somewhat surprised by my decision of leaving the kingship and seeking true-self as nobody in his opinion would let go of a lavish life and become a monk.

We laid down on the porch, under the vast blanket of the glittering night sky. Patches of clouds moved slowly, covering a portion of the sky at one moment and uncovering another part simultaneously. In between the cluster of stars and clouds lied the full moon, welcoming me to *Sarpanch's* house. I clearly imagined how father would have felt laying there.

"Vyas lied in the same bed as you are." *Sarpanch Ji* spoke.

"Tell me what happened that night, *Sarpanch Ji*," I asked.

He replied, "Vyas came here in this village to buy some seeds for agriculture. The wheat seeds he was looking for are only found here. Ganga's proximity makes this land more fertile than the land of your birth. And so, the wheat crops he wanted to cultivate in his village required those seeds which were sold in our markets only at that time."

"Yes! I saw some special and strange wheat crops displayed in one of the nurseries while on my way to your house." I replied, linking broken links of the puzzle in my mind.

Sarpanch Ji continued, "After having our dinner Vyas urged to sleep as he wanted to retreat to his village as early as possible in the morning. Your mother was pregnant with you and Vyas never wanted to leave her alone in that condition. I wished him all the fortune and luck, pointing towards the full moon that was shimmering its soothing pale light on both of us. What a co-incidence Eklavya, tonight as well is the full moon night!" He pointed his finger at the moon and continued,

"Vyas appreciated that beautiful night and his voice went down a few levels, indicating how exhausted he was. As soon as I turned in my bed, I heard Vyas saying *'What have I done? Oh, Lord!'* and he got up from his bed in a snap. All his sleep and exhaustion were gone! I was stunned to see your father's sudden reaction. Someone who always remained meditative and calm freaked out and sweated profusely that night. Upon asking, he told me that it was the night of your birth as per *Maha-Purohit's* predictions. I was worried because a storm just hit the region that evening, claiming lives and loss of property in both the villages. We both were concerned about your mother's condition. Vyas got ready to leave for his home right there, right then. It was me who reminded him that Ganga would not get any sailor in the night and that he must wait until early morning.

Finding himself unable to do anything to reach Sumati, Vyas spent the whole night talking about Sumati and regretted his decision of leaving her alone in that unsafe condition. He left early morning even before the sunrise. I never knew it was going to be the last day I saw Vyas." *Sarpanch Ji's* voice shook. I tried not to cry after listening to him but couldn't do much about it. I felt the warmth of my tears flowing down from the sides of my eyes and absorbed into the fabric of the bedsheet. The same night sky that astonished me with its beauty a few moments ago turned up blurred and lifeless. The moon seemed to be unwelcoming, making me imagine the night that shook my father's world forever.

"I will leave for Vaishali tomorrow, *Sarpanch Ji*," I told him about my plans but got no response from him. He was lost in deep slumber, snoring gutturally. After so many years of father's passing the mourning had not completed its course.

Somewhere deep inside my heart, lied a question of *'where have you gone?'* for all those who left me alone in this world.

Of course, there was nobody to answer that question. I never knew when sleep came over me slowly, and then all at once that night.

~~~***~~~
~~~

Maha-Purohit

After assisting Vyas in performing Sumati's funeral, I retreated to my home in another village. I decreased the number of my visits to Vyas' house and that village, fearing that one day, I will be caught for my crime committed. And whenever I visited Vyas after that, his neighbour, *Amma* treated me weirdly as if she knew something about me that I would not want her or anybody else in that village to know. Passive hate and disgust were visible in her eyes for me. Or maybe, it was only evident to me as I was indeed the culprit of Sumati's death.

Eklavya was very little then and as I often tried to pick him up, holding into my arms, *Amma* took him away from me. *'It's his nap time, eating time, playing time etc.'* were signature excuses she made every time I went near the baby. It was clear that she suspected me of killing Sumati but didn't tell anyone as she was not quite sure herself. But for me, her that level of suspicion against me was enough to call for *Amma's* elimination. *'It's better to kill two people and remain safe than killing one and being caught,'* I thought so under the influence of *Kali*.

I never visited Vyas after few months of Sumati's death. If *Amma* frequently saw me around Eklavya, she would have told Vyas about her doubt for what I did to Sumati, and expressed that I might try to kill Eklavya too. Her revealing that it was my herbs that caused internal bleeding in Sumati's womb would be enough to create a turmoil in Vyas' mind. And if by any chance Vyas or *panchayat* confronted me, I would have a difficult time concealing my crime. I was not sure, maybe I would be caught too, revealing and accepting what my intentions were and what I did, which I never wanted. So, it was indeed better to murder *Amma* and remain innocent than let her live and proven guilty of Sumati's death.

My hands were already in the dirt, and I felt no hesitation in getting them dirty once again. All I was waiting for was the time when Vyas would send Eklavya away for his education. Since Eklavya would already be away from Vyas, *Amma's* interference in Vyas' life would vanish or remain minimal. That, in turn, would give me enough cover from Vyas to execute my plan to kill *Amma* without getting caught.

In between those waiting years spent in my village, I visited the Vyas' village whenever I got an invitation to any social gatherings or ceremonies and saw Eklavya growing gradually. He was curious about learning fighting skills and showed a lot of interest in spiritual lessons at that tender age. I knew he was meant to replace the regime, he was said to change the times, and so, I never tried to harm him again as it would bring the wrath of karma on me as it did earlier.

It was after thirteen years of Sumati's death that Vyas sent Eklavya to the *Gurukul* built atop a Samrakuta mountain. I grinned at the play of destiny, as that *Gurukul* would make sure Eklavya earns whatever was needed for him to conquer the world. That Shankaracharya *Gurukul* was one of the best in the subcontinent. It was expensive to study there, as bright students from mostly wealthy and royal families across the nation went there to seek knowledge. It also had a policy of taking stringent admission tests before accepting anyone. I wonder how Eklavya passed their test just by being home-schooled from *Amma*. But then I realised he was Eklavya after all, he could do wonders.

After Eklavya was gone, I knew he will not return anytime soon from there. I had heard that students would only return after successfully completing three years of their initial studies. While I was sure that he would pass his courses with flying colours, yet even then he would only be able to visit back to his village after three years. Three years were more than enough for me to clear the only remaining obstacle from my path, *Amma*. The passage of thirteen more years had made her even older and weaker, and I discovered she remained depressed after Eklavya went away. This came to me as an excellent opportunity to cause lethal harm to her health, ending her life eventually.

As she began taking medications to cure her deteriorating health and depression, I replaced those medicines with mine. I persuaded and took *Vaidya* in my confidence so that he would give *Amma* to consume whatever I gave him. *Vaidya* initially questioned me about my herbs but soon fell into my trap of showing genuine concern about *Amma's* health and giving her some advanced and rare medications. I was the *Maha-Purohit* of the region, the senior-most authority among all *pundits* and astrologers. How could that *Vaidya* refuse my orders and retaliate my actions? He was a nobody in the village, a puppet in my hands.

Amma laid all the time on her bed, unable to get up, speak properly, eat or drink anything. My poisonous herbs worked well as *Amma's* health could not get any worse than that. It was then when I personally visited her house with the *Vaidya* and asked about her health just to pretend that I cared about her, and everybody else in that Village.

With the passage of days, I became more and more open about ill-treating *Amma*. I knew she told Vyas about my intentions and actions of killing her by giving poisonous herbs, but Vyas never took her seriously. Neither could anyone else in the village as *Amma* lost her sanity and became extremely tough to talk to. I knew by then that her end was near, and with her end vanished my fear of being caught. *Amma* was gone from this world. She died a natural death as they believed. Vyas was left utterly alone after that. He was vulnerable than ever, weaker and isolated from the world, lost profoundly in the grieving memories of his tragic life.

Eventually, people talked about his bad luck and showed sympathy for his family. I saw an opportunity in that talking of people which ensured Vyas' destruction. Without giving it a thought, I was all into my evil plan. I just deflected those talking about the bad luck of Vyas to the bad luck of the entire village, connecting all destruction to Eklavya's evil influence on the village.

I told them it was Eklavya who was cursed. I made them believe that the storm that hit the region before Eklavya's birth, mysterious death of Sumati right after her son came into this world, *Amma's* sudden death and now Vyas' health and mental condition getting worse, all of that occurred because Eklavya brought terrible omen on the village and its inhabitants.

Poor people always believed what I said. It all made sense to them. Not only that, I warned them to stay away from Vyas, and his child as whoever would come close to them will die. As I jinxed them day by day, Vyas lost his great influence on the community likewise. I didn't stop until Vyas lost control over his faculties permanently, he became insane, having no idea about who he was, what he was supposed to do, whom to talk to. Vyas was so volatile that he became the biggest fear among the children of the village. Insanity stole his mind, devouring all the wisdom he had and added lunatic traits in him. His condition was such that he feared his own shadow sometimes, left his house and slept on the streets, shouted for prolonged hours on women whom he earlier respected from the bottom of his heart and beat some children once.

*****

Fig. 14: Insane Vyas teasing one of the village-children.

Vyas turned up into total chaos in the village, attracting hate and immense denial of the villagers towards him. My motive of destructing Vyas' image in the village was accomplished well, and with the added bonus of *Amma's* death.

I retreated to my village after a few days, waiting for Eklavya to come to his family that was no more the way he left them. After two years and a half, I once again visited Vyas' village and made sure people abandoned him till then. It was also the time when Eklavya would visit his village.

Few days passed, and he didn't come. I thought he was informed of *Amma's* death and Vyas' condition, and in fear, he refused to visit his village. Even better for me! But after few more days of waiting, I accidentally met Eklavya. Instead, he accidentally saw me and called my name while I was passing through the marketplace near Vyas' home. I took that opportunity and put the blame for every tragedy on Eklavya.

He had grown up, but still naïve and innocent to believe everything I said about his cursed effect on all of our lives. He cried that day and lost it completely, something I already expected of him. He berserk initially at my explanation as to why everybody treated him differently that day, and a plethora of emotions burst out after that. He even met Vyas who had gone all mad, completely forgetting his only son. Something haunted Eklavya's mind after meeting his father that made him run away from where we were standing. That was the last time I saw him in the village.

I lived my days to the fullest - just knowing that now there was no Vyas to get conscious from, no *Amma* to reveal my identity to anyone and no Eklavya to get revenge from me. I lived a serene life that was unknown to me before. It was *Maha-Purohit* in the talks all over those two villages and no Vyas or Eklavya. My emotions fleeted, giving way to other ideas that helped me earn more money from the villagers. I exploited them in every way possible until there was nothing left with them to harness. But slowly and surely the reality began hitting me.

Over a few years, I became disoriented at everything I was earlier good at. I lost all my knowledge and practice of astrology and theology. My body became my cage, containing all evil that I did in my life. I realised the dangers of my deadly sins. I had sleepless nights almost daily, dreaming about Sumati laying dead in front of me, *Amma* telling my secrets in the *panchayat,* Eklavya killing me brutally after knowing what I did to his mother, grandmother and father. I hallucinated during the days, in between my talks and walks, seeing myself hung on a tree at the *choupal.* Many times, I ran barefoot into the wilderness protecting myself from the ghost of *Amma.* I was going crazy as I saw things that weren't meant to be seen by the eyes. My demons attacked me, as I feared my own shadow just as I made Vyas feel so.

Was it worth to live such a life? Not anymore. I had just prepared myself to call the *panchayat* and accept my crime before them. But destiny had some different plans for my revelation. I was called by the *panchayat* one day without me informing them about it. I went there thinking of it as a regular meeting that needed my inputs on some public issues. Little did I know that it was me who would be unmasked in public.

Upon reaching there, *Sarpanch* showed me a document *Amma* wrote in her last days, telling that I gave Sumati something that could kill Eklavya but instead made her womb bleed excessively, resulting in her death right after Eklavya's birth. The document revealed it was me who gave *Amma* poisonous herbs that took her life slowly and entirely.

I initially refused to accept all those accusations on me, but then *Vaidya* testified I gave him something unknown to be given to *Amma* regularly. *Amma* also warned everyone in that document about my actions against Vyas and Eklavya, which everybody then related to. I broke down with the weight of the world on my chest, accepting all that I was accused of. I never saw those villagers more stunned before as they were after finding me guilty of the murder of Sumati and *Amma*. I couldn't fall more in my own eyes, preparing myself for the death penalty I was going to get as punishment. My dream of seeing myself hanged from a tree at the *choupal* was about to turn into reality.

To my surprise, they all instead of hanging me decided to abandon me just as I did to Eklavya. People from another village were also present in the *panchayat*, claiming that they had burnt my house there in anger. Now I had no place to go to. I felt as if death was a comfortable compensation for my crimes rather than getting humiliated day by day in my own eyes. But I had to leave immediately from that village, assuring them I would never show my 'cursed' face to anyone in the town.

***

I went straight looking for Eklavya in nearby settlements. I spent my nights out in the wilderness, and days in search for Eklavya, the source of my karmic redemption. I got to know from my sources that he was in a cemetery on the other side of the river. Without any further delay, I headed for that cemetery which I had previously heard of. It had a graveyard inside its compound. It was slightly before midday when I reached the outer vicinity of the cemetery where his friend, Mahavir met me, testifying that Eklavya was there inside the ramshackle hut in between the cemetery and the graveyard.

I was initially refused entry by the old man, the caretaker of that cemetery, telling me that no one by the name of Eklavya lived there - not any, that he knew of. I doubted him and stayed near the area searching for Eklavya until I decided to go back again and check with that old man. To my astonishment, his behaviour completely changed the second time I visited his hut. He asked me to come inside and sit. It was not very long after I sat with the old man, telling him about who I was and how I knew Eklavya that Eklavya came inside panting. He was surprised to see me there and even more surprised to hear that Mahavir told me about him. Mahavir, a mysterious person who claimed to be Eklavya's friend but Eklavya never knew any such person ever.

I was there to confess to Eklavya about my sins, I was prepared to embrace even death that day. My evil-self shouted at me, scaring me of my insult and being ended by Eklavya, but I was not afraid anymore. I let it all out in front of Eklavya and the old man. There was a pain in my voice, anger for my deeds, shame in my eyes and repentance in my mind. My soul searched for redemption from the sins I committed.

Eklavya was as stunned to hear my confession as the old man was. Instead of chopping my head away from my body, he made me realise how ignorant and imprudent I was. He made me deeply regret my vice each day after that, and even now. He enlightened me that day, moving my soul from darkness to light, killing all evil that grew inside me under the influence of *Kali*.

Eklavya let me live to compensate for my sins. He spared my life so that I could do as much good as I could to bring back the real *Maha-Purohit* in me, to repent of my horrendous acts. He then told me to leave immediately before he lost his control over his anger. I did as he said. My inner-self was awakened after letting the truth out. Seemed as if I took a load off my heart and mind. It was me who put misery in Eklavya's life, I was the culprit for bringing tragedy into his life and his family's. Now it was time for me to put back on track whatever I could for him, and for his village. It was time for me to repay him for sparing my life. I would help him kill the evil in Rudraputra, it was I who would help him change the course of time and replace the evil regime. I realised I was the source of getting my predictions real for Eklavya. Because my involvement in Eklavya's fate for bringing the revolution in the kingdom was inevitable, I faced difficulties while determining the nature and future of Eklavya. That is why I struggled reading his horoscope and natal charts.

I walked out of the cemetery without knowing where I was going to go next, what I was going to do. As I was bound to help Eklavya change the way this world worked and end its sufferings, I developed a plan that would later bear its fruits. I headed straight towards the royal palace of Rudraputra. It had been decades since I escaped from the palace, fearing the punishment previous king was about to give me. It was now his son who ruled the kingdom.

His son didn't know a thing about ruling a country. I already knew he was only interested in women and alcohol. Finding it an excellent opportunity for myself to enter the system, I met the king of Rudraputra in his palace. As I explained everything to him in detail about my intentions to serve his kingdom as a royal astrologer, relating my ties to his father's times, he agreed to include me in his cabinet. To my surprise, he was so impressed with my talks and promises that he recruited me as the *Maha-Mantri* of his kingdom. Seemed like kismet helped me shape Rudraputra's future through Eklavya.

I was at the helm of the affairs in Rudraputra, but this time without any hidden and evil intentions in my mind. The sole purpose of my remaining life was to get the people of Rudraputra a suitable and well-deserved ruler who could kill the evil and restore the golden age.

Months went by witnessing a remarkable change in the way king's system worked in Rudraputra. I got the hang of his administration by then. The king was just there for show, and the real power vested in my hands. I always wondered about the reason why the kingdom still functioned despite being ruled by someone who under the influence of alcohol couldn't walk on his feet sometimes. I realised the royal cabinet had some noble people as the ministers of the state.

Together we made numerous changes in the policies so that people can benefit from it. I already knew when Eklavya reached that village in which he trained its people to fight bandits. I knew sooner or later he was to be in the palace, first as a prisoner and then as the king of Rudraputra. After about another month, Eklavya was brought in the palace in captivity. Not that he committed some crime, but we wanted to know what caused that holocaust in the village and how.

Earlier in Rudraputra, the king chose his cabinet, but not anymore. Plans were already in place of recruiting Eklavya as our king as it was the cabinet who chose their king in Rudraputra under my supervision. The dramatic and foolproof disappearance of the previous king brought the dawn of prosperity to the kingdom. Eklavya was appointed as the new king of the state. Together, we steered the nation and its people towards the golden age. With each day passed, witnessing Eklavya embrace the kingship of Rudraputra, I saw myself coming closer to attaining redemption.

After eight years of gloriously ruling the state, Eklavya wished to renounce his kingship to embark on his spiritual journey of self-realisation. I had the power to turn the wind around in Rudraputra, I could do whatever I desired, but how could I have stopped Eklavya from doing what he wanted. I was already under his debt of sparing my life. It was because of him that I stood there breathing in the air of peace in the kingdom.

But I couldn't let him go just like that! There was no other capable candidate except Eklavya who could efficiently rule the kingdom the way he did. All my hard work, all those years of misery, all the sins that I committed and all that the people of Rudraputra saw in the previous rules came down to Eklavya voluntarily giving up on his responsibilities. There was no way I could have directly stopped him from going, but I took his promise of returning back whenever Rudraputra needed him.

Unaware of the future at that time, Eklavya gave the royal cabinet and its people his word of coming back upon being called for any reason whatsoever. He suggested Bheema's son, Bibhatsu takes the responsibility of looking over the kingdom under my guidance. We all agreed, and Bibhatsu became the interim king of Rudraputra. Once again, the king was there just for show, the real power vested in my hands and I knew very well how to utilise it.

Apart from an emotional disconnect from Eklavya after he left the palace, everything flourished in the state under Bibhatsu's regime.

Until one night, when the evil dark took over the palace in its entirety. Mayhem prevailed all over, disrupting the order of the state. I tried my best to contain the cataclysm that *Kali* propelled in the palace, yet it was something beyond my might to fully control.

It was time for Eklavya to end his journey and immediately come back to Rudraputra. His golden kingdom howled in need of an *Avatar*, as it stood like a skeleton in the dark of that night and many nights after that. Rudraputra was doomed.

~~~***~~~
~~~

Acharya Virbhadra

After Pundir left the *Gurukul* there remained nothing for me to live by. I had taught there for decades, and that was enough of it. As the prophecy of Adi Shankaracharya became true and fulfilled, beginning with the admission of Eklavya in our *Gurukul* and accomplished with his sudden absence, there was nothing left for me to put my time into except for training Pundir, my disciple for the longest time ever.

Now that he was gone too, I wished to end my teaching career and live as a monk. I wanted to take *sannyasa*, leaving mountain-*Gurukul* and exploring some states nearby on foot just as Shankaracharya did, starting with Rudraputra. In between my want of ending my career and exploring the region, existed an urge to see Eklavya somewhere during my tour - the sooner, the better. I aspired to know what he did to change the course of time in Rudraputra. I witnessed a part of the prophecy getting fulfilled, but I fancied how.

Upon discussing my decision of taking *sannyasa* and leaving the *Gurukul* with Bhushan, I was surprisingly happy to know that he also thought of leaving the mountain-*Gurukul*. But he wished to retreat to our Kedarnath *matha* and not seek *sannyasa* then. He had desires of serving the *matha* for some more years before his retirement.

On one hand, I eagerly wanted him to accompany me on my exploration as we were always together since our childhood, while on the other, I prepared myself from inside for the separation that I knew was going to happen at some point in our lives. Kaushalacharya upon knowing our wish to permanently leave the *Gurukul* resisted, persuading and requesting us not to move. He remembered all good moments occurred in the *Gurukul* which Bhushan and I were an integral part of and reminded us both of those memories to allure us to keep providing our services. But we had decided that it was time for us to take leave of our teaching career there. Finding himself helpless and unable to do anything to retain us there, Kaushalacharya wished us the best with tears rolling out from his eyes. Those were the tears of love, belonging and mutual respect.

***

We taught for the last month in the *Gurukul*, waiting for Gandharv's chariot to come to pick us up. That last month was different than all other months I taught there. I put more than what I could while training students, I did better than my best to serve the *Gurukul*. Perhaps, it was the nostalgia that made me do all that in my last days of teaching life. That final month passed even quicker than the time we waited for Eklavya to come to the *Gurukul*.

Gandharv was on time as he had been since the time I knew him. When I first met him almost three decades ago, he was young, full of energy and passion, just as his horses were. Now, after three decades, Gandharv still matched his power and zeal to that of his horses. But the horses became old and weak with just enough force left in them to pull the chariot up and bring it down only once with snail's pace. Sadly, Gandharv turned old and weak just as his horses did.

While our way down the hill, I saw the chariot dragging barely with enough speed. Hooves that were once thundering became gentle footsteps for the horses, their synchronisation all mismatched, their fluffy golden mane had lost too much hair, those muscles that made them ripped and chiselled were mere lumps of flesh dangling in the air as they moved, those horses were not majestic anymore.

Bhushan and I remembered our trip uphill when we first arrived at the *Gurukul*. Everything seemed so beautiful and mesmerising then.

Everything was still as beautiful and as vibrant as it was three decades ago, but my eyes became old to sense it as accurately as it did back then. I might not look old on the outside, but my inside turned as weak as a fragile piece of glass. A sudden harsh flick of emotions could break it down completely. Gandharv recalled my joke to Bhushan about me pulling the chariot if he gets off from it and walks up top that made us all laugh like anything. All three cherished that joke even now, but our laughs were subtler and shorter this time.

Despite Gandharv's horses pacing as slowly as they could on their way down the mountain path, the valley arrived early that day. It should have taken some more time, allowing us three to recall and relive some past moments shared with each other about thirty years ago. But time showed no sympathy for our dismissal from the mountain-*Gurukul*, a place where we lived half of our lives. Gandharv stopped his cart, Bhushan got off carefully, and I followed him. We both hugged Gandharv, thanking him for his service and for giving us beautiful memories of the time spent with him. This time, we did not have any new clothes, or any souvenirs to give to Gandharv, just as we did thirty years ago. From the valley, Gandharv proceeded for his home, Bhushan towards Kedarnath-*matha* and I in the opposite direction to Bhusan, in search of Eklavya, the scion of Ikshvaku.

***

I knew where Vyas sent that letter in the *Gurukul* from as he mentioned his village on the envelope. Happy that I was not very far from Eklavya's home, I marched to his village, my first destination of exploration tour. After a few hours of walking and crossing the Ganga, I reached Vyas' village. I didn't have a clue where in that village Vyas and Eklavya lived. So, I asked many people if they knew their whereabouts.

Even though that village was mostly inhabited by Ikshvakus, nobody in the outer vicinity knew anything about Vyas or his son Eklavya. To some, their name seemed completely strange. I had no choice left but to proceed further inside that village and keep asking everyone who I saw on my journey about Vyas and Eklavya. Eklavya left *Gurukul* about fifteen years ago, and a lot changed in Rudraputra since then. That village too had evolved during those fifteen years, losing many older people, witnessing the births of many younger ones. I frantically searched for some similar faces in the village but couldn't see any. I realised it was hard to find Eklavya or Vyas in that village, indicating that they moved to some other place that nobody knew of. I roamed the streets from morning till noon but didn't have any luck locating Vyas' house. I wished he could have written his full address on that envelope.

As hunger prevailed in my stomach, I halted in the marketplace to buy some fruits for my lunch. The market was a busy spot in the village, located near the *choupal*, with a sea of buyers and sellers doing their business. Some sold merchandise, shouting out from their stalls to attract more customers while others purchased it, vehemently bargaining with the shopkeepers. In between those two kinds, existed another one that just did window shopping.

Numerous stalls lined up on both sides of the streets, showcasing their domestic products and services. A swarm of people hovered in those stalls, wanting to buy all that they could see. Amidst all that commotion were a fruits and vegetables stall adjacent to a pharmacy store. All fresh fruits on that stall were long gone, but I just wanted two bananas and two apples that were in plenty there. The pharmacy shop seemed to be a family business for generations as the old owner remembered every customer by name. I decided to give it a try asking the owner about Vyas or Eklavya.

As I entered the store, a distinct smell of all the herbs and pastes mixed together pricked my lungs. I never needed any medicines in my life, and so I had never been to a pharmacy store before that. If it were not for Eklavya that day, I would have stepped back the moment I smelled those Ayurvedic herbs and pastes displayed in that store.

I reached the counter, making my way through the crowd of customers wanting to buy all different kinds of medicines. I went to the owner that was sitting beside a young salesman standing, which I believed was his son. The old owner looked at me, closing his notebook which he was doing some calculations on. I greeted him and told him that I was looking for Vyas in that village. He struggled to remember my name which he never knew in the first place. So, I introduced myself and said that I was not from that village. He then asked me to come inside with him.

***

Fig. 15: Busy marketplace in Eklavya's village.

Inside was their office that had nobody except us both. He then told me something that I couldn't first believe. He said that Vyas died about fifteen years ago. He lost all his sanity, was abandoned by the people of that village and later found dead laying on the roadside one day.

I already knew that Vyas lost his wife as it was mentioned in his letter requesting Eklavya's admission to our *Gurukul*. What strange I got to know from that old owner of the pharmacy was that Vyas lost his wife to a planned murder and not an accident and he later lost *Amma*, an elderly woman who nurtured Eklavya after his mother Sumati died.

That owner was the only *Vaidya* in the village. He looked after *Amma* when she fell critically ill and eventually died because the *Maha-Purohit* of that village fed her poison through him, without him being aware of it. It was the same *Maha-Purohit* who planned to kill Eklavya even before his birth in Sumati's womb.

Since Eklavya was destined to born and change the course of time in Rudraputra, the poison killed Sumati instead. After listening to the *Vaidya*, I supplanted with bubbling anger. If that *Maha-Purohit* was there in front of me, I would have ended his life right there, right then. Such murderers don't deserve to live.

The *Vaidya* then told me about Eklavya becoming the king of Rudraputra. That news came to me as a sheer surprise – as shocking as me being wholly head-shaved, getting rid of my long matted hair like Shiva.

I forgot my anger for *Maha-Purohit* for some time, cherishing Eklavya's tremendous achievement inside my heart and mind. So, that was why he was born with prophecies, that was why Shankaracharya sent us to the mountain-*Gurukul* from Kedarnath *matha* to train him and to make him capable of ruling the state, our three years of training to him was enough to get him the throne of Rudraputra.

'What he would have done if he studied there for longer?' I wondered in between my conversation with the *Vaidya*. The old owner then suggested me to visit the palace if I wanted to meet Eklavya. I thanked him from the bottom of my heart for telling all that to me and immediately bought some more bananas and apples for my journey ahead to the royal palace of Rudraputra which was at a distance of few hours of walk.

I deliberately looked for what I wanted and never found it, and when I stopped chasing it, destiny gave that all to me in abundance. Life can become such sometimes, keeping you on your toes for the things you desperately want and rewarding you only after you surrender everything to it.

I walked faster than ever. I glided faster than Gandharv's horses for it was the time I would meet my favourite student, Eklavya, the king of Rudraputra.

'How does he look like? How am I going to meet him? Would they let me inside the palace? Would he care to remember me now? What if he ceases to acknowledge me?' All these questions perplexed inside my mind that lost its peace. This time, the chaos in my mind was sweeter than the order I always strived and vouched for. Pondering upon those thoughtful reflections in my mind, I never realised when the palace arrived. I could see that beautiful creation right in front of my eyes. A few more steps and I would be at its main gate that was bigger than that of the mountain-*Gurukul.*

Two guards stood there with their head held high, holding spears in their hands to safeguard the palace from people like *Maha-Purohit.* Those inglorious like him never deserved to be in such a legendary kingdom. I walked up to those men and introduced myself as the *acharya* of Eklavya in the mountain-*Gurukul*. Those men greeted me but never knew where Eklavya got his education and training from. So, they didn't let me inside the gate for security reasons, deeming that it was a false gig just to meet with the king.

I could have easily entered the gate if I were to use force, but instead, I requested them again to let me through. It was then when one of them said that Eklavya was anyway out of the state on his spiritual journey. It had been months since he left the palace, and Bibhatsu served the kingdom in the capacity of the king. They or anybody else didn't have any clue about where Eklavya went. All they knew was he was to go to Vaishali first and then to Kashi as per his initial plan that was in no way a guarantee to what he would actually do.

All my happiness and excitement submerged into the deep dark ocean of dismay. After getting so close to meeting Eklavya I got to know I looked for him at the wrong place. What could be more disappointing than that? Well, I was about to know that too.

***

Since it had been months since Eklavya left the palace, I was not sure where he would be then. He might have reached Vaishali and marched to the city of Kashi, he might have been somewhere in Vaishali, he might have been in Rudraputra, or maybe he was somewhere else that he didn't tell anyone about. The possibilities were numerous, but I had fewer chances of meeting Eklavya left with me. Being totally random about where to begin finding him, I proceeded to the kingdom of Vaishali, thinking that I would trace him down eventually by following his initial plan.

That way, my want of exploring the region on foot and meeting my student both would be fulfilled. As I walked towards the border of Vaishali, I watched my sabot taking steps on the rocky leafy *kutcha* road. Many bullock carts offered me the ride to wherever they treaded to, but I was not in a hurry for I never knew where my search would end and when.

By the end of the evening that same day, I reached a village that was at Vaishali-Rudraputra border. I went to the village's *Sarpanch* just to ask if I could get some shelter to spend my night there. The *Sarpanch* was a kind man, and he offered me to rest at his house. We didn't talk much that night as I slept early due to exhaustion. But next morning unfolded a series of some shocking information that he revealed.

Upon asking by the *Sarpanch* about what my plans were, I told him that I was looking for Eklavya, the king of Rudraputra. I didn't expect an iota of the information from him as his village was the very last village of Rudraputra and thus remotely situated. To my sheer surprise, he knew Eklavya and Vyas better than anyone. He was an old friend of Vyas and hosted him many times in his house in the past. I also got to know that Eklavya spent one night at his house before heading to Vaishali's Shankaracharya *matha*. I was amazed at the coincidence, for I got the most useful intel from a place I least expected to have such information. *Sarpanch* told me everything about Vyas and Eklavya that he knew. I then realised how helpless and weak the situations in life made Vyas and also that it was only Eklavya who could survive such tragic past, others would have given up on their life if they were to go through all that Eklvya went through.

My next destination was Vaishali's Shankaracharya *matha*, and without waiting much, I left *Sarpanch's* house. The *matha* was at a distance of a few hours walk from the border, and luckily I got some rides on my way that brought me there quite early than I had expected. Adi Shankaracharya's *matha* in Vaishali was much more significant and fancier than our mountain-*Gurukul*.

Unlike the *Gurukul* that was built for some other purpose and was later given to us in charity, Vaishali's *matha* was constructed by local *yogis* and proponents of *Advaita Vedanta*. A crowd of students of all ages dispersed from the big broad hallway of the *matha*. In that swarm of students, I saw one *acharya* making his way to the main chamber. We both saw and greeted each other from a distance. He asked me to come to his chamber. He was the in charge of the *matha* and headmaster for the students.

Upon introducing myself as former *acharya* of mountain-*Gurukul*, the headmaster looked at me with a thoughtful gaze. I realised he knew something for sure and asked immediately about his surprised reaction. It was then when he told me about Eklavya's visit there and his next destination that was the royal palace of Vaishali. I was as surprised to know the traces of his journey from the headmaster as the headmaster was after knowing that Eklavya was not only an alumnus of mountain-*Gurukul* but also the king of Rudraputra.

The headmaster requested me to stay at their *matha* for a day or two, but I politely refused his request, saying that it was utmost essential for me to meet Eklavya and that I didn't want to lose him after reaching so close. He understood my situation and told me the shortest way to arrive at the palace. What was the wait then, I headed to meet Eklavya who would probably be talking to the king in the royal palace of Vaishali about promoting trade between both the states or to introduce some policies that serve in mutual interest.

It was then when I reached the royal palace that the guards told me to go back as royal guards of Rudraputra took Eklavya back to their kingdom. I felt as if destiny played a funny game with my genuine desire of seeing my favourite student. I was always a step behind Eklavya in his journey, but I was glad I was at the right path. Sooner or later, I would meet him.

It had been better if I stayed in Rudtraputra, waiting for Eklavya to come back whenever the cabinet needed him or whenever he was done with his tour. I couldn't curse my fate anymore that day. All that journey, wait, and excitement cooled off as I promised myself it was the last time I was attempting to meet Eklavya. If he were not in the Rudraputra palace this time, I would continue my spiritual exploration without seeing him.

The royal guards of Vaishali's palace told me there was an emergency in the palace of Rudraputra, and it was that immediate reason why Eklavya had to end his tour and retreat to his kingdom suddenly. They didn't know anything else about that emergency, nobody in Vaishali did. This, in turn, motivated me and made me curious to know what happened in the palace there.

Only I know how I spent those two days of the journey back to Rudraputra. I spent one night at *Sarpanch's* house, telling him about something emergent that occurred in the palace. He initially wished to come with me to the palace but then dropped his plan, assuring that now Eklavya was there, he will bring everything back to normal. And sooner or later everybody would know what that emergency was that the cabinet called upon him immediately. I agreed to the logic behind *Sarpanch's* thought, but I had to go see him as soon as possible. So, I retreated for the palace the next morning.

Following the same old path, and this time taking a ride on a bullock cart I arrived at the palace. I saw the same two guards standing at the main door, with spears in their hands. Some signs of distress were evident on their faces, indicating that whatever happened should not have happened in the palace.

As I proceeded near the palace, those guards saw me from a distance and looked at each other, discussing something inaudible to me. Perhaps they planned on how to refuse my entry inside this time as Eklavya's presence inside the palace bounded them to give me some different reason than the previous one.

As suspected, I was denied entry by those guards again, saying that something tragic happened and nobody was allowed to visit the palace until further notice.

~~~***~~~
~~~

Eklavya

I woke up to the morning sunlight getting on my face as the veranda I slept in was directly under the sun. Chipping of birds and washermen's thumping of clothes on the shore was another reason for not being able to relax more. I wondered what kept me sleeping till that late as I always got up earlier than that. That instance of getting up late made me remind the day I left the cemetery. There was something in the coolness of the breeze in the old man's house that always made me sleep till late. I often woke up to the sound of the old man's work either in the graveyard or in the cemetery.

Although mountain-*Gurukul* always gave me the same relaxing vibe that urged me to sleep till late every day, yet *Acharya* Bhushan's classes of theology fascinated me more than sleeping in my dorm. I always remembered his reason for not letting us sleep after sunrise. He said, "he who sleeps for five hours a day is *yogi*, the one who sleeps for seven hours is a *bhogi* - the commoner and he who sleeps for nine hours is a *rogi* - the sick, the ill."

I was indeed a *yogi* in the *Gurukul* and a *bhogi* all after that. And now, I tried my best to regain the *yogic* attributes that were dominant in me in the *Gurukul* days. Self-control was required to seek *Brahman*.

Sarpanch Ji was not in his bedding. I wondered where he must have gone, but nothing came up in my mind as I had no idea about what his daily routine looked like. That day I was about to head to Vaishali, planning to visit the Shankaracharya *matha* in the capital and if possible the royal palace too. I was aware of the sour relationship between Vaishali and Rudraputra in the days of previous kings. But things were turning up well ever since I took charge of the kingdom.

While I prepared those plans in my head, I saw *Sarpanch Ji* coming in the veranda. "I am sorry, I never realised when I slept last night, cutting your conversation in between, I guess," he apologised for something I didn't even remember by that time.

"No, please don't apologise. I will leave for Vaishali now," I told him about my plans.

"What? You just came yesterday, son. Stay for a few days with me," he insisted.

"*Sarpanch Ji*, I will come again and meet with you soon shortly, but let me go this time," I requested while folding my bedsheet.

"If you were to go today only, you should have told me earlier. I didn't even get a chance to welcome you properly," *Sarpanch Ji* expressed his feelings about not being able to give me excellent hospitality, which he was completely wrong about. I wanted to clarify things before I leave.

"Well, last night I told you about my plan of leaving for Vaishali, but you slept by then." He looked at me with raised eyebrows, and we both laughed at the situational juxtaposition.

After eating my breakfast with *Sarpanch Ji*, I left for Vaishali's *matha*. After a few bullock cart rides, a lot of walking and some rests in between I reached Vaishali's *matha* in the evening. As *Sarpanch Ji*'s house was already near the Rudraputra-Vaishali border, I knew I would reach the *matha* that same day.

Adi Shankaracharya's *matha* in Vaishali was more prominent and fancier than our mountain-*Gurukul*. Nobody there knew that I was the king of Rudraputra. And neither I wanted to reveal my identity to them. They knew me as a *Brahmin* scholar wandering around the city. I introduced myself as one of the alumni of the mountain-*Gurukul* and got a warm welcome there. I was asked to stay there for a day or two and then leave. I struggled to accept their request but then agreed as I wanted to see how their system worked. I was curious to compare it with our education system.

One of their *acharya*s took me to all the classes and introduced me to the kids. I was glad to meet with so many students that were going to shape the future of the subcontinent later on. I saw my childhood in those young learners. *'Some of them would be like Pundir, some might become like me, others like Acharya Virbhadra or Bhushan and remaining might become like their acharyas,'* I speculated.

***

It was the very last hall which *Acharya* took me to that rang some bells in the back of my mind. As my eyes quickly glanced at all new faces in all the classrooms, I found a familiar face sitting there on a mat. Apparently, that child didn't recognise me because of my entirely new and strange look. Moreover, it had been a decade since we last saw each other. As soon as I saw him, I got another valid reason for staying at the *matha* for a day or two. Though I kept my emotions and eagerness off my face, yet I was all bonkers at the sight of him.

He was Tara's brother, who helped her save my life in the tribal captivity. He had grown up, too old to be called a child and too young to be an adult. His early teenage look put me in doubts about his identity a few times, but I just knew he was Tara's brother. How could I forget him staring at me in pity when I was being dragged for the execution. Only he and his sister didn't want me dead that day, rest all cheered at my helplessness. I remembered that face very well. What was he doing there? How did he come there? I wanted to ask everything from him. But at the same time, I didn't want to tell them all about myself and put that child in trouble. I had to do something to get some time with him after the class was over.

I requested the headmaster about letting me choose some kids and talk to them about their experience in the *matha*. I told them it was only for the sake of curiosity and to see if anything new has been added in the curriculum after I left the Shankaracharya *Gurukul* on the mountain. Without hesitating, the headmaster approved my request, and I chose few students from several classes, taking him too. Upon asking, I got to know his name was Chandan and he came to the *Gurukul* about half a decade ago, running from his home. After some superficial chit-chat with other students, I called off my interaction with them but asked Chandan to stay. Nobody had any clue about what I was doing. Chandan stood there, glancing at me in desperation as he too wanted to go with his friends but couldn't because of me.

"Hey! Chandan, I am Eklavya. How are you doing here?" I politely told him about me.

"You have told us your name five times ever since you came here. I get that you are Eklavya. Can I go now?" he innocently made me realise what I just did. I then realised he would not remember my name because he was too young at that time. So I tried making him remember the incidents of the past.

"I will let you go if you tell me how did you come here, escaping your tribe in the jungle?" I said. He looked at me with frozen gaze, wondering how come I knew about his tribe in the jungle.

"Who are you? How do you know about my tribe?" he was curiously worried and almost forgot about going back with his friends now.

"I am that man whom you and your sister, Tara saved a decade ago. I am Eklavya, the king of

Rudraputra," I answered only to find him stunned with his eyes wide opened and both hands covering his mouth so that he doesn't utter anything loud out of surprise.

"What are you doing here? What have you become, Eklavya? Tara never returned home after running into the jungle with you..." he put forth a series of questions, making me realise that I wasn't the only one to have questions and expected me to answer before I could get anything from him.

"I have now become the king of Rudraputra, I am on my spiritual journey. That is the reason why I shaved my head and wore these *yogic* clothes. Tara was with me all the time. After we escaped from your tribe, we engaged in a bear fight in the jungle. Tara saved me from that bear too. But I couldn't save her from the bandits. She died fighting with the bandits one night when I was in another village helping one of my old friends." I told him everything I could.

"What? Tara died?" he confirmed.

"Yes, almost a decade ago."

Chandan went in shock but didn't cry then. His little age at that time of my escape with Tara and separation of ten years form his sister was enough to detach him emotionally from Tara. But sill Chandan knew he lost his sister whom he loved so much, and that is why he stood there still. I hugged him gently and felt his tears wetting my long peasant-style top. I let him cry to release his emotions. After that, he told me everything about his escape.

***

"Few years after Tara was gone, I was left alone in the tribe. She took my promise of not telling anyone what we did there to save you and gave her word that she will come back for me. I kept my promise and never told anyone, not even *Maa* and Father about that, but she broke hers and never came back to get me out of there. *Maa* and Father died in an epidemic, leaving me alone to a relative whom I didn't like. Finding myself trapped in their home and in monotonous life of the jungle, I ran from there one night and came here. I thought if Tara can escape why can't I. I never knew if I was going to reach anywhere but knew I was going to get out of that tribal culture, and I made it here. I begged, borrowed and stole on my way, but I reached here," Chandan panted.

"It's okay, perfectly alright," I consoled him.

"Have you ever been saved by anyone except Tara before?"

"Yes, my friend Mohammad once saved me from drowning into the Ganges," I replied while pondering upon his sudden weird question. I didn't want him to know about my suicidal thoughts, and so, I told him I was drowning instead of my feelings of jumping into the river to end my life.

"What? You know *Acharya* Mohammad?" he was even more surprised this time.

"Well, I have met him a couple of times before, but I don't know much about him. Do you know him? Where does he teach?" I felt as if I found a direction to a long lost treasure. My years-long want of getting to know about Mohammad was about to get fulfilled. I waited eagerly for Chandan to say something. Instead, he grabbed my hand and dragged me somewhere, I followed along. He took me to another empty classroom and asked while pointing his finger towards a portrait hung on the wall,

"Is this your Mohammad?"

It took a moment or two to get that portrait registered in my mind. My eyebrows arched for the sky, startling me at the very sight of that wall-hung figure. How could that be possible? The calmness I showed to Chandan outside after seeing that portrait couldn't reflect what I felt inside.

I was almost paralysed, staring at Chandan one moment and the picture in another moment. My words left me, I wanted my lips to move, my tongue to utter some words but I couldn't do that. I almost fainted when I saw Mohammad's portrait there. The man who had been the biggest mystery of my life was there in the classroom, and a child apparently knew much more about him than what I knew. I recalled his appearance, and it exactly matched the one on the wall. Same height, facial expressions and his neck-hung bag too!

"Yes! Yes!! He is the one... Who is he?" I stammered.

"He was the alumnus of Shankaracharya's *Gurukul* in Kashi, Banaras as they now call it. He died two decades ago. *Acharya* told us one day when my friend asked him about who this person was and why his portrait was hung on the wall..." Chandan replied, leaving me numb after hearing that Mohammad died almost twenty years ago.

'The person who saved me from ending my life in the Ganges about two decades ago was the spirit of Mohammad? Wh...What??' I thought in my mind.

"Do you know how did he die?" I further asked Chandan to see if I can get more information.

"*Acharya* told us that he died in the Ganges after his boat sank accidentally when he was going back to his home from the *Gurukul*. And since then his spirit has been protecting anyone and everyone it could from drowning in Ganga." Chandan smiled as he knew by then that the friend I talked about who saved my life was Mohammad's spirit.

"Everyone here and in Banaras knows about him," Chandan further added. Now everything made ·perfect sense in my mind.

'*Mohammad died in an accident in the Ganges, and his sudden unnatural death kept his soul from attaining liberation. And since then it is preventing more deaths from happening in the river. Mohammad's spirit saved me that day and took me to the cemetery. No wonder he knew everything about the old man and his wife's grave! No wonder he appeared out of the blue and passed by while singing that song when I lost Maha-Purohit in the jungle after he was sent back by the old man. He changed his name to Mahavir because he didn't want me to look for him after Maha-Purohit told me about his meeting with him. Mohammad knew if Maha-Purohit told me that he met Mohammad, not Mahavir, I would have rushed outside immediately to find him. Oh my god! Mohammad is a ghost!*'

Fig. 16: Chandan pointing towards the wall-hung portrait.

I felt a spine-chilling sensation in my body, realising I had been seeing, talking to and meeting with a ghost for so many times in the past. He even told me the story of self-control while on that ferry. How could I never recognise he was a ghost? He never looked like one, he never sounded like one, and he never felt like one. Though I didn't know what a spirit looked, seemed or felt like. What is happening in my life? I broke down after perceiving how strange and mysterious my life had been. Chandan pacified me in his own unique way by gently patting on my shoulder.

"I don't want to study here anymore. Can I come with you to Rudraputra?" He asked.

"I am not going to Rudraputra now. I am going to meet the king of Vaishali, and then I would head to Kashi. I don't know when I am going to go to Rudraputra," I explained so that he could understand I didn't want to take him along with me.

"I can also go meet the king and then visit Kashi with you," Chandan was adamant. I knew he had nobody left whom he could call his own. His situation was almost like mine was, nobody to call my family, nowhere to go. Clutched in the emotion of belongingness, I told him to come with me.

He was happy to have my permission, I was glad I gave it to him.

***

The next day, I told the headmaster that Chandan wanted to go with me, and I had no issues in taking him along with me on my journey. The headmaster was aware that Chandan had no parents, no siblings and nobody whom he could consult before sending Chandan with me. Also, he knew Chandan came to his *Gurukul* on his own. So, there was no harm if he now wanted to get out of the *Gurukul*. The headmaster allowed me to take him with me. Chandan and I both thanked him and proceeded ahead towards the palace of Vaishali to meet the king.

We shared a lot of things with each other. Chandan further told me about his past days after Tara left him, I shared with him my dramatic story of becoming the king of Rudraputra. At first, he didn't believe me, thinking I was good at making stories. It was after I told him about how my parents died, he believed me, admitting that nobody would ever make fake stories of their parents' death. Chandan was a kid, after all, he had got his own believing mechanism.

The palace was not far from the *matha*, and we were about to reach there. Chandan was more excited than me about being included in my spiritual journey. After walking a little further, we both saw the palace that reminded me of my palace in Rudraputra. I imagined how mine looked like, thinking what *Maha-Purohit* would be doing and how Bibhatsu managed the kingdom. The uniform that Vaishali's royal guards wore was similar to that of my guards. *'Perhaps the king stole the idea from Rudraputra's army,'* I thought suspecting Vaishali's king of copying every good thing and idea from Rudraputra.

It was after reaching near the boundary of the palace that I saw those royal guards, mounted on horses and approaching towards me were from Rudraputra's army and not Vaishali's guard. It was too much shock in one day. Sometimes, I felt like it was all happening in my dreams. I told Chandan that those were my guards. He was even more excited now.

"Greetings! King Eklavya," the commander greeted me. I acknowledged his salutation by nodding in affirmative.

"How come you all are here? Is everything alright in Rudraputra?" I asked.

Chandan simultaneously spoke to me "How did they find you? Did you tell them you were coming here?"

I looked at him, smiling and choosing to ignore his question. Even I didn't ask about them finding me because as a king, I knew my army was excellent at search and rescue operations. Besides, one can never know what *Maha-Mantri* of Rudraputra was capable of doing. During my months-long tour, I even suspected of being followed and tracked by my men quite often. Who knows what the real reason behind them knowing my whereabouts was, and I didn't bother about it much.

"*Maharaj*, there is a situation in the capital. *Maha-Mantri* requested your immediate presence in the palace. Please come with us!" the commander said.

"But it has only been a few months since I left the kingdom and I haven't even started my *sadhana*. I can't come with you," I justified my answer. The commander looked at me in the eyes, something that he had never done before and said,

"I am sorry to hear that *Maharaj*. But let me remind you of your promise that you gave to *Maha-Mantri* and the cabinet that you will immediately return if called for any help," the commander reminded me of my assurance that I gave to *Maha-Mantri* before temporarily renouncing the kingship.

"I remember it very well, commander. But at least tell me what happened? Why my presence is required in the capital?" I asked once again. Even if he didn't answer my question, I still had to go as per my words to my cabinet and *Maha-Mantri*.

"We have not been told anything, *Maharaj*. Even I am wondering what happened and in such sudden notice. I hope nothing serious occurred. A little after midnight yesterday, *Maha-Mantri* called a very brief meeting and sent us to find you and bring back to the palace as soon as we could. We went to every single house you went to, every street you walked on, talked to almost everyone you talked to and finally reached *Sarpanch's* house who told us about your arrival to Vaishali's palace and now here we are standing in front of you right before the royal palace of Vaishali. Please come with us," the commander confessed his null knowledge of what happened in Rudraputra, and I could tell from his voice and his eyes that he wasn't lying to me.

I immediately told Chandan to mount with one of our soldiers on the back of a horse. And I climbed on another horse that was brought for me from the palace. Our convoy galloped towards the royal palace of Rudraputra as fast and as swiftly as it could, passing plateaus, brooks, hills and jungles with tremendous pace. The distance that took me so many months to travel on foot would take a few hours to cover on the horses.

I was worried about the safety and security of my people in the kingdom, whereas, Chandan enjoyed his ride on the back of the horse.

As I entered Rudraputra, I saw everything perfectly normal. I saw people doing their daily business, I saw marketplace filled with consumers and producers, I saw children playing, elderly people roaming around. The city looked as subtle as it should look. Nothing was as I expected it to be. This, in turn, made me even more worried and restless.

I knew something severe happened that *Maha-Mantri* didn't even let anyone know outside the palace to prevent any chaos in public from happening. I patiently rode my horse towards the palace, eagerly waiting for the time that would reveal whatever sinister happened in the royal palace.

~~~***~~~
~~~

Pundir

Gandharv's chariot bumped a lot descending the hill that day. As I sat facing the direction which the chariot was moving in, I leaned abruptly towards those three students sitting inside, facing me. Though I held the support bar as tight as I could, yet I felt either I or the bag hung around my neck was going to fall on their faces. This lone thought made me laugh whenever I saw their faces during that trip down the hill. I didn't care what they thought of me, but it was a bit awkward to me.

A while ago, I was not even interested in looking at those students who already stared at me as if I was their culprit. And now I had no choice but to see their drooping-rising cheeks every time a bump came under the wheels. I felt like scolding Gandharv's horses, but it wasn't their fault either. The rocky path was rough that day. Last night's heavy rain and a thunderstorm in that area of the mountain brought debris on the road, Gandharv told us collectively without anyone asking about the reason behind that rough ride.

That bumping and thumping continued for some more time, and with amplified intensity until it became unbearable for the cart to pull the weight downhill. A sudden and robust thud occurred, and one of the rear wheels disassembled itself from the chariot, rolling towards the edge of the mountain trail and fell. One student sitting in the corner hit his head on the support bar that I held. Horses stood still and stopped their neighing entirely as if they already knew it was going to happen and indeed deliberately wished for the breakdown of that cart so that they could get some time to rest.

A weird silence conquered out of shock that accident brought with it. For a moment I was all glad that I sat comfortably and not leaned on those students, but then I realised what has happened and jumped off the chariot to inspect everything from outside.

Gandharv wailed, repenting the loss of chariot's wheel but was glad that he, we all and his horses were safe. Something much worse could have happened in a blink of an eye. Unable to go anywhere until Gandharv installs another wheel to the cart, we stood in the middle of nowhere. And to my sheer surprise, he didn't have any spare wheel with him that day. Not being able to do anything to help themselves, those three sulked vehemently.

There was no way anyone could have come to that hilly trek to help us. Moreover, we couldn't even tell someone that we were stuck. And even *Gurukul* didn't have any chariot wheels, so going back there to seek help made no sense.

Gandharv suggested us all to retreat to the *Gurukul* as it was not very far from where we stood and spend one more day there. Meanwhile, he was to go down the hill and bring back help the next day. He told us that we should be able to reach the *Gurukul* in about an hour on foot whereas, the trip down the hill would take anywhere between six and eight hours depending upon our speed. Besides, the jungle near the lower mountain range in the valley had wild animals that might attack vulnerable and exposed people walking on foot.

I had already decided I wasn't going back uphill. So, I said I was coming with him downhill no matter what. I didn't care about walking for eight hours or wild animals. Gandharv then asked those three about what they were going to do. All three of them went up and waited for Gandharv to pick them up the next day. One hour of an uphill climb and a delay of one day seemed more comfortable to them than six hours of the downhill trek and saving of a day. To each his own, who was I to judge them on their decision. So, we just took their food and water that they brought with them for themselves and sent them uphill.

It was after the three were gone far from us that Gandharv grinned, carrying mischief in his eyes that told me something I could initially not understand. I asked him what was it that made him smile even after incurring such an expensive loss. Gandharv then pointed towards both of his horses, and I immediately got what he thought of doing.

Since those three were gone and we two left there, Gandharv untied his horses from the cart so that we both could go downhill riding on their backs. Such a great and smart thinker he was! We reached in the valley even before we expected. While on our way to the valley, I asked him why he told us to go uphill in the first place. He then justified that he could not discriminate between all four of us. And that it wasn't a wise idea to offer his horse to only one of us. Besides, he never wanted to leave us all stranded there. If he had told us about using the horses before, who would have gone back to *Gurukul* then, he looked at me while making a point. Now that those three went uphill wholly with their will, it was easy for Gandharv to include me in his plan. That proved Gandharv's integrity towards his duty. He was an Ikshvaku after all, how could he haven't shown his integrity towards his service?

****

The horses galloped rapidly with synchronised footsteps, tearing into the barren pathway. I mounted on the back of one for the first time in my life. As they were meant to pull the cart and not carry anyone on their backs, Gandharv didn't put the seat on them. And so, I felt the bones and muscles of my horse quivering underneath as he strode. Both were as naked as a jaybird. The frame, the saddle and everything else attached to their body enhanced their beauty, but it was never that they didn't look beautiful without all that. The thundering of their hooves, fluffy manes dangling in the wind, rippled muscles that perfectly crafted their chiselled bodies and everything else made those stallions look majestic.

I could have continued the journey to my home after coming downhill, but that would have left Gandharv alone to figure out how to fix his chariot up there, which I didn't want. And so, I offered him my help. He denied initially, thinking that it wasn't fair to make me postpone my plans because of him, but then I made him realise what if I too had gone up with them, I would have delayed my plans even then also. So, I better be spending my day helping Gandharv rather than waiting for him to arrive in the *Gurukul* the next day. He then agreed to take my help, finally. I felt relieved, and at ease, as at least this time I volunteered to spend my day helping him rather than being made to exhaust one at *Gurukul* due to that accident.

After we came down, we looked for a shop where we could buy one wheel at a reasonable price. Wherever we treaded in the valley, people stared at us, making me realise that only we two mounted on the back of horses. But knowing that we couldn't afford to walk on foot as it consumed more of our much-needed time to reach places that day, we remained seated on the horses for the most part of our lookout for the wheel.

Soon after, Gandharv bought one from a carpenter, and we quickly ascended uphill on those horses. Though it seemed, we did everything quickly, yet it took us a lot of time to descend, look for a shop to buy replacement wheel and then ascend uphill to the chariot.

It was already late evening when Gandharv finished his installation of that wheel. Horses were reattached to the frame, making the cart good to go anywhere as it was before. It was again a situation of a dilemma for both of us. Either we could climb up and bring those three students downhill with us the same evening, or we could go down, take some rest and Gandharv could come back again in the morning to take them down the hill. If we were to go uphill and then come back, it would already be late night by the time we reach downhill. Then where those students were going to go in the middle of the night?

After pondering upon all possible aspects and doing his calculations, Gandharv proposed that we go downhill, spend the night at his house and then in the morning he would come back to pick up those three, and I would leave for my village. The proposal sounded great, and I agreed to it. We then resumed our journey down to the hill, this time with a little less pace as it was dark, and we didn't want any other accident to happen. And for obvious reasons, neither he nor I wished to die that night.

We had only covered the half distance till the night entirely prevailed. The same mountain and its path that looked vibrant and blossomed during the day turned dead into a place of witch-crafting with the trees that stood still like a coven looking out for any passer-by to be their prey. Soft neighing and hooves of the horses echoed around the valley, creating a menacing trance. It was not precisely fear that I felt, but I was reasonably upset travelling on that trail after dark. All sense of logic and self-control that I learned in the *Gurukul* vanished. What remained inside was an elevating primal fear that triggered a pre-fight, flight and freeze mechanism. I imagined different versions of the fight scenes with random opponents and very well mastered my moves in case any wild creature or spooky person or anything comes on our way, posing a threat to our lives. But all that practice of combat remained contained inside my mind only. I was not sure if I would do such brave acts if a real situation occurred that night.

Gandharv, on the other hand, was just concerned about the safety of his chariot and horses from tripping on to any rock, stone or anything that was brought there by the storm last night. Perhaps his frequent commute on that hilly route made him fearless of the surroundings, or maybe it was his eagerness to reach home and see his wife and kids that subsided his fear.

Humid chill supplemented the tantric vibes coming out of the jungle that ran on one of the sides of the path along with us.

"How far?" I asked. Gandharv said,

"You won't die here. We will soon be home," and chuckled, making fun of my alertness. I could only have ignored his statement at that time.

Soon after, several white and yellow, bright light dots appeared, indicating that we were close to the settlement. A rush of contentment ran inside my body, so much relieving that I tilted my head skyward and thanked whoever was up there, far beyond the million glimmering stars in the sky.

Gandharv was married and had two handsome boys who together opened the door when we arrived. Seeing me standing on the door at that weird time of night, the younger one quickly ran inside the house without even noticing his father standing beside me, while the older one stayed, looking at me agape.

***

Fig. 17: Gandharv's sons strangely looking at Pundir.

I froze at the door for a few moments, unable to decide what to do next until Gandharv asked me to follow him inside. After introducing me to his wife and kids, he explained everything to her about being so late that day. We then ate dinner prepared by Gandharv's wife. It was after a long time that I ate something different and tastier than what I had been eating there in the *Gurukul* for ages. There came a time when I was so disinterested in eating *Gurukul*'s tasteless food that I thought it was my taste-buds that developed an impaired sense of taste. Luckily, I was wrong as that food at Gandharv's house melted on my tongue.

Boiled rice, lentils, sizzling cottage cheese and many more delicacies lied in front of me waiting for my mouth to hog them all. I pleasantly consumed a little more than I generally could and appreciated Gandharv and his wife for their warm hospitality.

Kids had already slept by that time. Soon after, we all prepared to sleep. Gandharv's wife and kids were in one big room while Gandharv and I lied in another, a bit smaller one.

"I will leave early, even before the sunrise," I said. Gandharv insisted me to go after having my breakfast. I told that I didn't want to get late as it was another eight to ten hours of the journey on a bullock cart and on foot to my village, and there layed Ganga and a jungle in between.

"If this is what you want, so be it. I will also leave around the same time for the *Gurukul*. I will give you a ride till wherever I can," he said. I was curious about the education Gandharv gave to his kids.

"Your kids are now grown-ups. So, which *Gurukul* are you sending them to?" I asked with excitement. He didn't answer for a while. I looked at his face that, in the dim light of lamp hung on a pole appeared deeply submerged into the ocean of countless memories. I wondered if I had asked something utterly personal to him, or something that scratched off an old scar inside his heart.

"Are you alright?" I wanted to make sure everything was alright.

"Nothing, your question just made me recall something from the past... I... I once went to a *Gurukul* by the Ganges to get my kids admission there. That *Gurukul* was close to our home. And so, my wife and I wanted our children to go there and not the mountain-*Gurukul*. With the advent of *Kali* in the region, *acharya* there asked for the huge amount of money that I couldn't give them.

I begged a lot, but nobody listened to my requests and made fun of me in front of my kids. My kids freaked out as the staff kicked me and told me to get out of there right then and return only when I have enough money for the admission of both my kids.

The amount was huge, and I knew I was not going to have that much money ever. I went out of there, my kids followed me. Finding myself not being able to feed my family properly and educate my children in the *Gurukul,* I loathed myself in disgust.

The shock that I got after they kicked me in front of my kids made my skin crawled. I sneered to hide my emotional outburst and told my sons to go home. After they were gone, I headed straight to the shore to end my life. There was no reason for me being alive if I couldn't even nurture my family. I hated myself, I cursed my grotesque fate, I surrendered to my miserable life. I stood on the river-bank and saw Ganga flowing with tremendous rage that afternoon. The brutal might of Ganga's icy water seemed to be the perfect coffin for me. Without looking back to my retreating kids, I folded my hands, and with my eyes closed recited last prayers.

***

'*Om Shanti, Shanti, Shanti, Om.*' I was about to jump into the deep swirling waters of the Ganges but a voice killed all my impulse of ending my life.

"*Excuse me! I am lost, could you please help me find my way home?*"

I turned back and saw a tall man with a small bag hung around his neck stood a little far from the shore. He called himself Mohammad..."

I wake up to the chirping of birds the next morning and immediately realised I slept last night mid-way my conversation with Gandharv who was still sleeping. I debated if I should wake him up as he told me about his plan of leaving around same time as me for the *Gurukul*. Founding him snoring gutturally, I did not wake him up, instead put my stuff in my bag and quietly left the house.

On my way walking to my home, I wished I could have stayed up longer last night to listen to Gandharv's story of his life being saved by Mohammad. I wanted to know who that man was? What and how did he save Gandharv's life, what happened after he asked Gandharv about his way and everything that happened that day, but last day's exhaustion took entirely over me without me even knowing of it existing. The secret of Mohammad remained a secret to me forever.

At times I thought of going back to his house and ask him to continue his story from where I couldn't listen to it, but that idea seemed too wild and naïve to be acted upon and so I kept on walking until I got a ride on a bullock cart that dropped me right before the only jungle between Gandharv's village and mine.

I got off the main road and walked on a rough terrain that took me to the jungle. The trails ended right before where the forest began, leaving me confused about the directions to follow. I stood there for a moment, allowing my mind to analyse whatever it could about my actions. I picked up a fallen branch of a tree and kept it with me, thinking it would serve as a weapon in case I ran into anything wild in the wilderness. Although I was not sure if that thin branch would kill a tiger, lion, bear or even a snake for that matter.

The jungle was dense in some areas and sparse in others, making it difficult for anybody to keep track of their path and time. I had heard in the past about many deaths of people lost inside the jungle due to a lousy sense of directions while remaining inside it.

Some were even found dead laying a few footsteps away from the boundary of the village surrounding it. Sadly, they didn't know they were that close to getting out.

Years ago, when I came to the *Gurukul*, Father escorted me to the valley, guarding me against any potential harm. And when I visited home, we were a group of students, unlike this time when I was alone. Father very well knew about the geography of the jungle. He walked it many times before for work purposes. I was excited to see him after so long, only if I could manage to pass through that jungle and cross the Ganga safely. I realised if I had stayed there where I stood running my mind about what was going to happen after stepping into the jungle, I would have never reached my home. And so, I just went inside it and prepared my mind to face anything and everything that may stand against me.

As I entered further inside its denseness, the sun that sparkled in the village lost its shine into the tightly packed trees in the jungle. Shrubberies, fallen branches, scattered brittle-brown leaves and dried fruits reached me from everywhere as if I was some sacred master of their fate that when touched, would change their lives by turning them alive.

The path was ancient and untouched, telling the stories of its loneliness since ages. The jungle existed there without a cause, creating problems for commuters like me.

It was my idea that if followed correct path and at the right speed, the jungle would be gone in just four hours. Now all I had to do was follow the correct path and maintain the right pace, which was easier said than done. I heard the chirping of birds atop my head, pecking wood. By that time, I had my feet and legs bitten by bugs and pricked by sharp sticks and thorns. No matter how careful I was, the jungle showed no mercy.

I passed through muddy swamps, countless swarms of bees and mosquitoes that followed me till very far, the slippery floor covered in dead remains of trees and animals and the noisiest chirping of crickets I had ever tolerated. There moved mostly small animals like squirrel, goose, frogs - too many of them, peacocks, and those I never saw before and knew nothing about. I wished I don't come across any big ones that day. Not that I can't kill them to save myself, but it was a lot of work for me which I never wanted to do as I still felt tiredness in my body from last day's hustle.

I imagined what Gandharv must be doing at that time of the day. Probably, climbing uphill to get those brave-hearts who in fear of being killed by animals in the lower range jungles headed swiftly for the *Gurukul*. I chuckled recalling the scene and Gandharv's cleverness of using horses to come down. And then my smile was all gone the moment I realised I would not get to eat that delicious food anymore during my journey until I reach home. Perhaps, I should have stayed there for breakfast, I concluded.

***

Few hours passed, and I knew I followed the right direction and without encountering any wild animal in the jungle. The sky and the sun appeared from the top of the gigantic pine trees, indicating the end of the wilderness was not very far. The air was fresher with the fragrance of leaves, loams and wild fruits as compared to the humid, damp air in the denser jungle.

But something was not right. It came to me as a shock that it was almost evening by that time as the sun reached very near to the western horizon, proving that the jungle never cared about my time or anybody else's. The journey that I expected to be for only four hours took almost triple of it.

Not regretting anymore what had already happened, I was glad I came out of it alive. But then the ground slipped under my feet, I froze as the blood inside my body diverted away from my gut to my muscles, when I saw what I never wanted to come across in that jungle. It was a lion, a big scary one apparently sleeping or pretending to sleep and reminding me that the wilderness was not over yet.

His golden mane stretched from ear to ear, and the padded claws covered lion's one eye. He perfectly camouflaged himself between the golden-brown trunks of deodar trees, fallen dull yellow leaves and scattered chunks of sharp sticks. I was so close to him that I could hear the breathing with his ribcage rhythmically rising and falling. Or maybe my sense of hearing just got better with rising fear. Once again, fright found me and sat on me like a suffocating mask. The terror that I faced while coming down the mountain last night was peanuts as compared to what I felt standing in front of that sleeping monster. Even the subtlest of the movements could wake him up annoyed, something that I thought of several times in my head while standing there but never wished it to become real for even once.

***

Fig. 18: The beast sleeping in the jungle.

I was excellent at archery and sword fighting, but neither I had a bow and arrows, nor did I have a sword to fight. I then remembered - such fear seeped inside me that I suddenly remembered… I was also great at unarmed fights and one to one duels, but one to one fight with a real lion? I was not so sure about that! Warm blood in my veins coursed through my body, pushing me to run as fast as I could. It was my enlightened mind that made me realise I could never outrun that beast. I wish *Acharya* Virbhadra trained me to be an excellent runner too.

'I must recommend athletics for all the students in Gurukul once I get out of here in a single piece,' instead of making some useful plans my mind thought such random ideas out of the blue. Well, what else I could have done then? I was too afraid to fight it, I was so sure that I couldn't flight it and freezing was not going to help anymore. I laughed at my kismet and helplessness.

'Was it for such a dramatic end that I saved one day by climbing down to the valley yesterday? Those three were lucky to have stayed in the Gurukul. Is it the end of my life? No! No! No!'

I regained my conscious and gathered the courage to slowly walk past the lion that showed no sign of alertness.

Slowly, steadily and one step at a time I prowled like a frightened cat that might soon be eaten by another cat in the light of sheer bad luck. There was a small pit that appeared to be dug by some animal to hide. I could have gone around that pit, but it would have taken a few more steps, steps that I couldn't afford to waste, so I decided to go over it. No matter how carefully and skillfully I pounced over it, the landing was rough and noisy because of dry leaves and bushes on the floor of the forest. I looked immediately where the loin was sleeping and found he wasn't asleep anymore but stood right where it rested.

It was at that moment, my gut dissolved inside, wanting to vomit out everything inside it only if I had eaten anything that day, which I hadn't. The lion saw me, I indeed was looking at him for who knows how long. He then opened its big mouth and let out a roar from deep within that was heard miles around. In return came few more roars from a distance, indicating his call was acknowledged by his pride. He then walked about around me not paying much attention to my still standing body.

There was a hope that the lion was not hungry. If he had been starving, he should have attacked me by then. I held still in this hope that he will go away from me just about any moment.

I heard some roars again that seemed to be approaching near. Now it was confirmed that that the lion called others so that they all could lodge an attack on me together. That is how they kill their prey in groups. I couldn't afford to lose my life without even trying to fight back. I didn't want to die after reaching so close to the end of the jungle. So, I prepared myself to charge on that beast before his other friends would come and tear me apart.

My senses were at high alert - eyes wide opened and fixed at that lion, neglecting every other thing between him and me - its colours became brighter, every sound my ear heard was louder, heartbeat became fiercer and chest filled with as much air as it could fill. I wasn't the same Pundir as a while ago. I was the warrior who earned the headband in the *Gurukul*, I was the fighter who fought *Acharya* Virbhadra and won over many other staunch combaters, I was a devotee of Adi Shankaracharya, and I was that lion's death that gave him ample time to escape, but it didn't go. And that's why he was going to die right there right then for his ignorance.

I knew my strength, and it was a matter of a few powerful stabs on his head with my knife that would kill him. I also speculated few scratches, maybe some bloodshed too for myself. But in the end, I knew I could finish him. I ran towards him with my fists clenched and almost instantly stopped. I saw him going in the direction where the roar came from, he didn't even look at me again.

'*Wh…What??*' I was strangely surprised. Seemed as if that big cat trolled me, made fun of me, almost made me piss in my *dhoti* and just left. He just went without even looking at me again, leaving me extremely disappointed and self-fooled. Without waiting for a second, I charged ahead with tremendous pace and without even looking back. Now layed mighty Ganga that after going through all that in the jungle seemed a cakewalk to me.

As I reached on the shore in the evening, the sailors were long gone. I already prepared my mind while I was in the jungle that I might have to swim through the river. It was a short walk to my village after crossing the river. So, without thinking much I entered the water, feeling an expected chill in my body. I was worried about the wall hung portrait of Shankaracharya that I kept inside my bag rolled up nicely, getting wet and destroyed. But I could not help it.

Ganga seemed to be as vast as the jungle was but being able to see the other end of it was much relieving. It gave me hope that I was going to get across the river quickly. The cold water numbed the scratches and pricks on my legs and feet that I got in the jungle. Felt as if mother nature after giving me hardships in the forest pacified me in the river. My ears that heard distant sounds clearly in the jungle got blocked as the muddy water of the river entered them, turning everything soft and silent. I couldn't even hear the displacement of water while I swam, but it didn't matter as I was glad seeing the other shore coming nearer with each stroke I made.

I was at the other end in no time. My body wanted to relax on the banks, but I couldn't wait anymore out of excitement to visit my village, my neighbourhood and my family after so many years. So, I almost ran until I reached my village.

Though it was late evening yet, it wasn't that late to see empty roads in the village. The sailors should be returning to their homes from the shore, farmers back from their fields and others retreating from wherever they were during the day. The children should be playing on the streets with other children, women should be doing their chores, visitors and merchants should be retreating to their places. But I saw none of them, nobody, not even any cattle on the streets. Shops were empty, houses laden with thick layers of dust and the *choupal* longing for someone to come to it and discuss different matters.

I was scared, scared if bandits attacked my village. But then I didn't see any bandits too. And if they were gone, then there should be people gathered outside their houses, repenting their losses and asking each other about theirs. But I saw nobody. For a moment, I stood still and thought if it was the right village I came to. Where could have everybody gone? I ran towards my home faster than a racing horse, passing by the empty marketplace that once was a river of buyers and sellers. I saw some huts shattered, many broken bullock carts, debris piled up in patches as if nobody cared to dispose of them for years and some boats with their wood dried up. I was glad my neighbourhood looked familiar, with few windows opened and lamps illuminating their insides. My house looked alright too.

I didn't care about knocking on the door and opened it with force only to find out it was not locked from inside.

My house had some strangers inside it. It was a family of four, screaming at the sight of me. As if I was the one who intruded their property. I was to grab that man's neck and squeeze it so tightly until he suffocates to death, but I didn't want to do that in front of others who I think were his wife and children.

"Who are you? Where is my family??" I panted.

"Who are you?" the man asked me instead. I was worried and in shock.

"This is my house! You are inside my house! Where is everybody, why is my village abandoned?" I told him who was I.

The man, after knowing that it was my house calmed down instead of stressing out. Several wrinkles on the forehead of that man's wife relaxed after listening to my answer.

'Surely these are not thieves otherwise they would have attacked me or rushed outside or done anything that they could to protect themselves from the owner of the house they stole,' with this thought in my mind I calmed down too, waiting for an answer from the man.

"We are tribal people settled here for almost a decade now."

"What?" I couldn't get my head around what I just heard.

"Where has everybody else gone then?" I further enquired.

"Most of them are dead. Remaining few sought refuges in the capital of Rudraputra," he replied. I felt the floor slipping under my feet.

"Dead…what does it mean? Dead how??"

"About a decade ago bandits from our tribal region attacked one night in the village. A fierce battle took place between the villagers and them. Few bandits who escaped that massacre and returned to our tribe said the villagers fought until they killed as many bandits as they could. It had never happened in the past that villagers retaliated to the loot. They would simply cooperate and give whatever the bandits asked for. But that night brought wrath upon the bandits too, as they lost almost everyone from their gang. The king of Rudraputra trained your villagers to fight those attackers. He was the one who manipulated them to fight for their rights, resulting in their deaths while fighting those goons.

This village turned into a graveyard with dead bodies of villagers and bandits laying everywhere, on the streets, in the pond, in the well and everywhere else.

Later, the royal army mass-cremated them all. Since then this village is abandoned. We never saw those bandits returning to the tribe and one day after few weeks had passed, went to see what happened. It was then when we discovered that the entire village was abandoned. We needed resources and shelter, and so, those few of us who were left in the settlement came here and have been living here since then. We are not bandits, we are just commoners like your villagers were. But we belonged from the same area as those bandits were. Not everyone in our tribe was a bandit, we are nomads. I am sorry for your loss. We can live somewhere else…," he explained.

That man spoke something I couldn't listen. All I saw was his mouth moving too slowly to be normal. I sat on the floor with my mouth open. Streaks of saliva poured down from my open mouth, but I never realised it until it fell on the palm of my hand. Tears rolled down the cheeks, I shivered in cold, such cold was even more freezing than the chill of the river.

I felt nothing was inside me, nothing needed to be outside too. I looked at the door thinking about my mother and father, asking them in my mind where were they and the only answer I got was the creaking of that door loosely hinged and moving with the breeze. Every second took peace from inside me one chunk at a time, leaving me collapsed just like those huts in my village were.

My family was robbed and killed while I prepared myself in the *Gurukul* to protect them from those bandits. *Maa*, father, my neighbours, friends and everybody else in the village died while I embraced the beauty of the mountain-*Gurukul*. Had they not retaliated the loot that night, they would have been alive. Why did the king push them to pick a fight with the bandits? My family and everybody else in the village always cooperated and gave all that those bandits wanted. All they had to do was to keep doing that until I was back. *Maa* and father knew that I went to the *Gurukul* after spending five years at home only to get better at fighting so that I could train all of them to get rid of those bandits and their atrocities.

The grief surged intensely with each breath I took. There was an emptiness in my heart, a strain of nothingness that killed all the bravery, integrity and wisdom I possessed. It became hard to breathe, shoulders swamped under a massive weight of distress that was slowly killing me. I stood up and went outside my house, walking in the direction of the royal palace. I didn't see the prevailing dark outside, I didn't care how would I reach the palace, I just wanted to go inside it and ask the king for his justification.

***

One more day of the continuous journey on foot passing through a smaller settlement, a hill and a vast barren land brought me to the capital city of the kingdom of Rudraputra. It was midnight when I saw the royal palace glittering in the light of a thousand candles and lamps. Few guards walked on its roof. I didn't know where I stood or what was around me, the moment I saw the palace I knew I had arrived at my destination. Immense exhaustion drenched my body, hunger and thirst almost killed me. I remembered my free fall on the ground that night, making me unconscious.

When I woke up, the sun was about to set in the sky. It was the evening of the next day. Nothing came to my mind when I saw some water stagnant in the ground except drinking all of it as quickly as I could. After I drank it like a thirsty wolf, licking the ground with my tongue that didn't taste a thing from the last two days, I felt as if it was the best day of my life. That stinking stagnant water was no less than elixir to me that day. Now I had to find something to eat.

I walked straight into a house and asked them to give me anything they had to eat. The host family was equally shocked after seeing me in their house as I was after intruding in there. They gave me the food in abundance, and I walked out as quietly and peacefully as I entered. I sat under a tree and gulped it all like a demon feasting on blood. My face was all soaked in the curry, hands were dirty, and food scattered all around that place. After I finished eating, I stood up and went to the same house I intruded earlier.

I was back in my senses by then and chuckled at the closed door that was widely opened before when I broke into it. I knocked, but nobody opened. I knew I could smash that door with the slight use of force, and I did it. Now they screamed as though I had taken out flesh from their bodies. I ignored them and put back the empty utensils which they gave me food in and drank some fresh water. They were quiet now. I also gave them my bag that had all the clothes, taking out the rolled-up portrait and my knife as a token of appreciation, folding my hands before them for their involuntary help and exit through the broken door.

I reached very near the royal palace and hid in the bushes. I must confront the king that night, as I couldn't afford to wait until morning. I knew the guards would not let me inside at that odd time of the night, so I had to enter it in stealth. I desperately waited for the midnight when the security of the palace would be minimal, leaving behind fewer guards to slaughter in the line of their duty.

It was the night of the new moon. Millions of stars could not compensate for the silver-pale light of the moon if it were in the sky. It was almost pitch dark, but a thousand lamps and candles illuminated in the palace shimmered the region more than the stars in the sky could. I saw few guards pacing smoothly on the roof of the palace, two stood at the main door that was too high to climb. I didn't know why they had guards on that door. I figured out it was easy and safe for me to enter from the rear entrance which was slightly difficult to reach but once there, I could have easily climbed the not so high walls. I quickly and discretely revolved around the building until I saw the back door which was not as high as the front one. As the back of the palace was already mostly guarded by the trough of the plateau on which it was situated, no guards were watching it.

My only problem was those who watched from the roof of the palace. I carefully noted in my mind their pattern and timing of patrol they made on the roof and realised it took them few moments to reach the end of the roof, leaving the middle area unguarded. It was that short time duration that I had to climb the wall in. Not only that, I had to jump off the wall safely and run until I get to a safe place, away from the line of sight of the guards on the roof. Also, there might be some more guards inside the compound that I wasn't even aware of.

There was too little time and so much to do with the tremendous risk involved. I never feared death, but I didn't want to die before confronting the king of Rudraputra, the murderer who killed *Maa* and father. I was way too nervous than what I was on the day I had to fight *Acharya* Virbhadra.

'I pledge before you all to finish those who killed and continue to exploit my village and its resources. Those who come even close to my family in bad faith will lose their life. I can't let Kali span its wings so easily, not until I am alive… Despite being a Brahmin, I won't hesitate to do the tasks of a

Kshatriya, just as Lord Parashurama did to avenge the killers of his father…'

The pledge that I took before the consortium on the night of my final debate in the *Gurukul* recalled itself in my mind. Now that those bandits were already dead, killing my family and people, my next culprit was the cruel king of Rudraputra. He was the one who annihilated an entire village. He was the one to be punished, he was the one to be avenged, he was the one to be killed! And I made sure he got what he deserved.

~~~***~~~
~~~

Acharya Virbhadra

Rudraputra Royal Palace: Present

As I entered the hallway to court with *Maha-Mantri*, I saw a swarm of people who I believed were the royal staff of the palace, standing in a group outside the main entrance of the court. The hallway was bigger than the neighbourhood of Eklavya's village, including the marketplace.

A servant saw us coming from a distance and ran towards *Maha-Mantri*.

"*Maha-Purohit*, he is breathing…he is alive!" said the man while addressing *Maha-Mantri*.

'*Maha-Purohit*??' I thought in my mind. Not being able to contain my curiosity even at that saddened time I looked at *Maha-Mantri*,

"Did he just call you *Maha-Purohit*?" I asked.

"Yes, I am the *Maha-Purohit* of Rudraputra. But now I work mainly as the chief minister of the state. It's a long story," he replied while looking at the crowd that came nearer as we saw our steps taken on the shiny marble floor of the hallway.

As his words fell in my ears, my fists clenched in anger. It was the same *Maha-Purohit* who killed Sumati, put *Amma* to eternal sleep, tried and later succeeded in destructing Vyas. That eunuch was the same person who made Eklavya's life devastating to live, the same eunuch whom after knowing his sins I had thought of killing the moment I see him. And now he walked right beside me. My heart exploded inside my chest, debating if I should serve the justice right there right then. My eyes went red and moist, looking directly at the swarm of people but not really perceiving anything except giving *Maha-Purohit* what he deserved.

I could have killed *Maha-Purohit* before his eyes could blink. But wondering about how he became the chief minister of the state deflected my anger at him. I couldn't believe I walked next to a murderer and hesitated to give him what he gave to those innocent people – death. Several more questions draped my excitement of meeting Eklavya and the fear of witnessing whatever gore happened, resulting me controlling my lethal anger on *Maha-Mantri* of Rudraputra.

'If he holds such high place in the state, he must have done something extraordinary. If Eklavya despite

knowing that this eunuch is the murderer of his father, mother and grandmother let him live and even included him in his cabinet, then he must have deserved to live. If the royal guards resisted me each time from entering the palace but then let me pass upon one non-verbal command of this murderer, then I shall let him live for now and not do anything under the influence of my anger.'

I analysed the possibilities of sparing his life and found it reasonable to wait until I get to see the bigger picture.

As we reached those staff members standing outside the entrance of the royal court, we were given our way to the inside. The courtroom was as vast and big as the hallway, alluring its visitors to embrace its enigma. Neglecting the big windows laden with thick clear glass, velvety smooth long curtains hung on the bars, hundreds of comfortable chairs glued with exotic stones, the mighty throne made up of decorative metal and polished wood crested with gems and gold and soft furry carpet with an ideal courtroom scene embroidered on it, my eyes stuck at those two guards who lied on the floor, crying discreetly with the pain they were in.

Royal *Vaidya* treated them with herbal pastes and dressings with the help of a young boy who looked like a student of Adi-Shankaracharya *matha*. One of the guards was conscious and cried, recalling and blabbering the deadly encounter he had last night while the other was semi-conscious and writhed in pain. Their face bled, arms and legs all swollen, patches of blood stained their clothes that were visible from the broken armour they wore on their chests. Seemed they had a fierce fight with a hungry lion in the jungle. The breakage of their armoured vest was enough to tell the force that beast exerted on their chests that left me wondering how they could both still breathe. It appeared to be the sheer luck that saved them last night from being butchered to death by that animal.

I still hadn't finished speculating what might have happened to those two severely wounded guards, but *Maha-Purohit* asked me to come upstairs to the bedroom of the king. I couldn't catch up with his statement. It took me by surprise as to why he would tell me to come to the bedroom of the king. I then understood that what I just saw in the court was a glimpse of that unfortunate event that occurred last night. The real gore I was told about was upstairs in the bedroom of the king.

Fig. 19: Virbhadra & Maha-Purohit on their way to King's bedroom upstairs.

Concerned about the scene I was going to see, I asked, "What is upstairs, *Maha-Mantri*?" to which he didn't say anything, and we both climbed the stairs. I saw a distinct sense of disturbance on his face which was not there downstairs near those wounded guards.

'Sure enough, there is something much more disturbing than what I just saw,' I thought while following *Maha-Mantri* on the staircase that was about to end in a hallway to the bedroom of the king.

The upper floor was the exact replica of the lower level with the only difference of being bedroom instead of the courtroom there. As soon as I stepped to the hallway. I saw another swarm of people standing outside the door of the bedroom of the king. But those weren't the staff members or civilians but the royal guards, guarding the entrance to prevent any unauthorised access.

If I were alone, I would have no chance of getting through that garrison of guards. Even if I were to use all my force, it would have been much difficult and stressful for me to enter the bedroom. The upper floor itself was inaccessible to the royal staff and majority of the ministers.

As I took steps in my wooden sabot on the marble floor, it clattered as to the hooves on the rocky road, making everyone aware of our arrival there. As we came closer to the room, the distress on *Maha-Mantri's* face became more profound. He looked into my eyes, cautioning me about the arrival at the scene so that I could brace myself to witness the gore. Subtle hints were evident from the bloodstains on the walls and floor in the area near the bedroom entrance. The royal guards made way for us to enter the room. What I saw there was unexplainable and nothing less than bloodshed of the millennia if not less.

For a few moments, I couldn't believe what my eyes saw. And then I felt something sticky forming in my mouth that made me throw out everything that was inside my gut. I vomited at the very sight of someone whom I didn't recognise, laying on the bed.

Had I known it was that I would see there, I would have retreated from the outside of the palace door, without even asking to let me in twice. If that were the answer to all my questions of Eklavya being called upon immediately in the palace and what made Rudraputra doomed, then I would have lived with those questions forever as they were in my mind – without any answer to them.

If a hungry lion had attacked those severely wounded guards downstairs, then this was bloodshed caused by something as powerful, outrageous and destructive as tens of those hungry lions, all at a time on one person. Being wholly baffled after seeing it, I lamented on the floor wailing.

As soon as I was on the floor, I saw *Maha-Purohit* already sitting beside me with his head bent down in shock. Though he already saw it earlier, yet every time he saw it, he felt the same disgust inside. Beside *Maha-Purohit*, I saw whom I had been eagerly waiting to meet, but not in that condition. I saw Eklavya who was already staring at me who knows from when. It took me few moments to realise it was him because of his completely shaved head and *yogic* attire that was soaked in blood. The sensitivity of the scene was such that it never let me notice my surrounding.

Eklavya cried in distress. I could see a tinge of surprise on his face for a moment after he saw me there as it was totally unexpected for me to be present in the palace. But again, the sorrow of that tragic incident took over the bedroom with all of us howling.

Eklavya's hands were red in blood, and some pieces of human flesh were stuck on his head. Perhaps he went too close to the bed in shock, trying to wake the king up.

That bed had Rudraputra's king Bibhatsu laying in it, dead. It was Bibhatsu who was murdered, instead butchered last night in his bedroom. His one eye lied outside the socket, wholly crushed and other was closed. The bed was soaked in his blood oozing slowly from his intestines that dangled out of his stomach. Something thick reddish pale in colour exploded from the back of his skull, probably the brain matter.

If Bibhatsu's face was covered, no one could identify that it was him only by seeing his slumped body. Arteries from his limbs stuck out like so many tangled wires, his rib cage was visible too. It seemed like even tens of hungry lions would not have done that with his body, what had been done already.

Many brutal stabs with some sharp object like knife were made on his stomach that was cut open and corrugated. Despite being so many scented flowers in the room, a smell of blood and raw flesh prevailed.

I stood up to go out of that room as I couldn't take it anymore. I vomited once again and saw something filthy already on the floor, which made me throw up even more. As I turned around, I saw someone and felt the ground slipping under my feet.

It was sheer torture on my brain to soak so many shocking events all at once.

I saw Pundir confined in thick iron chains hanging around his neck, waist and tied to his hands. Six guards held those chains, preventing him from moving.

On the floor laid a portrait of Shankaracharya and his knife with which he slaughtered Bibhatsu. It was the same knife he brought with himself to the *Gurukul* when he was young. If I knew that knife would do such annihilation, I would have destroyed it or taken it from him right when I saw it hung around his waist at the time of admission. Pundir had seen me entering the bedroom before I could see him and so, his head was purposely bent down in mortification for what he did.

No wonder only he could kill someone that brutally. I froze where I stood, seeing both of my students at one place but none in the condition I expected to be. One was caged in chains, and other wailed in sheer suffering.

Perhaps, Pundir was alive for that long only because he was Eklavya's friend from the *Gurukul*. If it were anybody else, the first thing Eklavya would have done is to tear apart their head from the torso.

At that moment I wished I had gone with Bhushan to our Kedarnath *matha*. Eklavya, *Maha-Purohit* and everybody else waited for the only executioner in the capital of Rudraputra who was expected to prepare Bibhatsu's dead body for cremation. I wondered if that executioner would be able to see and then assemble that scattered piece of flesh, bones and blood slowly soaking its fluid to the fabric of the bed.

By the time he arrived, our eyes were dry, leaving us unable to cry anymore. We all had accepted the brutal death of Bibhatsu and prepared ourselves to cremate his body.

The executioner hesitated initially to touch the dead body of Bibhatsu at the sight of its barbarous condition. But later, draped the body in few layers of white clothes and prepared its bier.

The people of Rudraputra gathered outside the palace, waiting for us to bring the dead body out. Many joined us in our walk to the cremation ground. I still contemplated all that happened with me in the past few days after I left the mountain-*Gurukul*, pacifying my mind that soon things will be alright in Rudraputra and in the lives of its people.

~~~***~~~
~~~

Fig. 20: Bibhatsu, the fallen king of Rudraputra.

Epilogue

Time

Pundir no matter how righteous he was in his own opinion, spent the rest of his life in the prison of Rudraputra. After realising that Eklavya did the same thing in good faith that he had planned for his village to get rid of the bandits, Pundir forgave Eklavya and served his sentence in prison without any resistance and malice for unknowingly murdering someone innocent. His imprisonment was justified in his own mind, and he would rather be at peace in the captivity than being in conflict outside the prison for all his life.

Whereas, not being able to release Pundir for he had committed a heinous crime though unknowingly and with a legitimate reason in his mind, Eklavya once again felt like an orphan of the storm that shook his life since he was born. Pundir was his oldest and best friend after all. How could he have seen such a mindful and wise friend spending his days in the prison, hoping to see the free world someday that would never come? How could he let Pundir suffer alone in that empty black space with no windows, no doors, no sunlight and no other person to talk to?

How could he let such a fierce warrior confined behind the rusty, sticky iron bars, just as a lion in the cage?

Eklavya could have done anything to prevent Pundir suffering further from any misery, but his principles never let his best friend go free of the crime he committed. Eklavya was the king of Rudraputra and leader of his people first and a friend after.

To speak his heart out and to make Pundir's days less heartbreaking, he visited the prison every morning and evening as a friend and not the king to meet his still best friend. That was all he could do in the line of justice to prevail.

Chandan was made the king of his tribe upon the recommendation of Eklavya. Initially, the tribe was reluctant to accept Chandan as their king because he ran away from the tribe. But their king grew older and was in search of the right candidate to lead the tribe. Chandan's education, maturity and Eklavya's recommendation and trust on him were more than enough reasons for the tribal people to accept Chandan as their king.

Bheema grew even older and learnt to live without his loving son, Bibhatsu. He knew nothing could bring back his only son who was butchered to death without even doing anything to deserve it. But he crumbled into the sands of time, accepting whatever destiny had to offer him.

Pundir's imprisonment eventually became enough for Bheema to soothe his heart for the compensation of his son's loss.

Acharya Virbhadra, on the request of Eklavya and *Maha-Purohit*, agreed to spend his remaining days in the palace, assisting them all with the administration. He often missed Bhushan and the Kedarnath *matha*, waiting for Bhushan to visit him in the palace someday.

With each sun rising on the horizon, the palace felt more optimistic about its future. The enemy in the form of evil surrendered before the grace of Eklavya for he refused to be powerless, to put down his belief in the power of truth and righteousness. Rudraputra and its people recovered slowly from their tragic past as the rays of hope conquered the darkness of despair and evil.

Peace, love, strength and prosperity were restored in the kingdom. Everything seemed to become as pleasant as it was in the days of Eklavya's kingship before he left for his spiritual journey.

The royal guards stood at the hinged massive metallic door of the palace with their heads held high in pride. Once again, the world headed towards the utopia, coming out of the clutches of *Kali*.

Sumati and Vyas were happy to see their son conquering the evil, just as *Maha-Purohit* predicted about three decades ago. *Amma* often appreciated Mohammad's efforts of saving Eklavya from taking his life in the Ganges. Whereas, Mohammad often thanked *Amma* for homeschooling Eklavya at a tender age.

The old man and Tara talked about how Eklavya evolved from a helpless boy to a mighty warrior. Tara was glad to see her brother leading the tribe. And Mohammad cherished Eklavya's headstrong homecoming to Rudraputra.

They all were amazed at the contribution *Maha-Purohit* made to bring everything back on the track after getting his life spared by Eklavya as he had gone through a remarkable transformation. They all were sure that he would get redemption from his sins in the afterlife.

No human alive was there to see Sumati, Vyas, *Amma*, the old man, Tara and Mohammad relive their moments of life, for they all sparkled among the million other stars in the night sky.

And I witnessed all of that from the beginning until the very end with you. I saw everything just the way you did because I was born along with the *Brahman*. I was there when nothing was, I am here when nothing is, and I will be present in all years to come.

I am time, and I stood still to tell you the story of Eklavya, the scion of Ikshvaku and the king of Rudraputra prevailing in *Kali-Yuga*, a tiny fraction of my span. An era that would soon cease to exist, welcoming the golden age with its both arms wide open.

Embrace yourself for the journey to *Sat-Yuga*, an era which is yet not born but almost there to come. An age where everything seems as it seems to be.

~~~***~~~
~~~

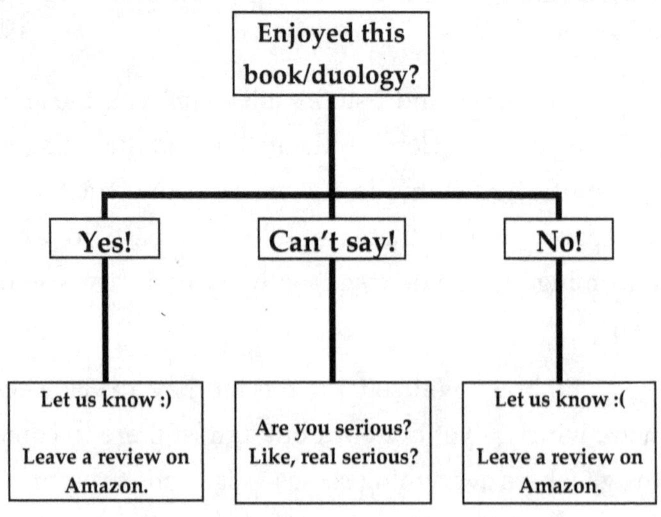

Enjoyed this book/duology?
Yes!
Can't say!
No!
Let us know :)

Leave a review on Amazon.
Are you serious?
Like, real serious?
Let us know :(

Leave a review on Amazon.

www.ingramcontent.com/pod-product-compliance
Lightning Source LLC
LaVergne TN
LVHW091450170726
843492LV00001B/127